The Writings
of the Masters

Enlightening lessons for everyday life
from the Masters and Angels,
as interpreted through an impartial
witness and given with love of the One

Deborah Hill

Copy Editor: Denise Hmieleski
Photo Illustration, Design and Layout: Deborah Hill, Online Creative, Inc.
http://www.onlinecreative.com
Photograph of Deborah Hill: Phil Skinner

Library of Congress number: 2003095367
ISBN: 1-59330-021-2

Published by Aventine Press, LLC
45 East Flower Street, Ste. 236
Chula Vista, CA 91910-7631, USA
www.aventinepress.com

For information or ordering:
Malaya Creations
5269 Glenridge Drive,
Atlanta, Georgia 30342-1354. USA
www.malayacreations.com
or **www.writingsofthemasters.com**
877-462-5292

To those who have taught me,
supported me, loved me, stood by me:
Masters, angels, guides and teachers,
my friends and family,
my editor whose support was invaluable.

To God, who is all and ever more.

TABLE OF CONTENTS

PART ONE:

Writings Extracted from Dialogues

People ask me if I was always psychic. The answer is yes, but I didn't realize that no one else I knew was—until about five years ago. Throughout my life I've realized that when I talked and acted from my place of understanding, I basically shocked people. It was cute when I was a child. As a one-year-old, I was thought of as adorable and precocious because I could talk; as a two-year-old I could say things that were intelligent and insightful; and as a three-year-old I could give insights into situations. But from four years old on I was seen instead as a "know-it-all." I learned to not speak my truth out loud.

It was frustrating for a four-year-old psychic trying to communicate and find a place to fit into the world. I'd see people do things that I knew would not work. They would lie about themselves, and strangely no one else knew they were lying—sometimes not even them. I would point the lies out and would be severely chastised. It's understandable that my family and friends felt this way. I would say things that offended others because I thought I was pointing out or referring to the obvious. I would try and force my will, even at four, because I knew that whatever we were doing would not work.

I remember driving to Ohio to visit relatives. We were supposed to stay with cousins. We took the wrong route and ended up arriving late, to the chagrin of the entire family. I had known when we turned onto the wrong road; I had felt it. But imagine how my parents reacted when their four-year-old started giving them driving directions. They became irritated and angry, thinking, "There she goes again, saying something with authority about what we're doing when she obviously has no understanding of the situation." Yes, I could tell what they were thinking, too.

I remember another situation. I was with my mother when she met a highly respected doctor. My mother was and is very attractive, and he wanted to impress her. He began to tell her about all the people he'd helped, the surgeries he'd done, and how successful he was. Some of what he said was true, but much of it was glorified and altered to impress my mom. I could see this as plainly as I could see the color of his suit. After he finished his little oration, I said with curiosity and interest (and a little belligerence because he was lying to MY mom—whom I felt like protecting), "Why are you making up stories?" Of course, my mother was horrified and chastised me in front of the doctor for saying such a thing. After a couple years I learned to be quiet, to not say what I saw, and eventually to actually doubt my own understanding and insight.

I felt so alone because of this. I felt like an alien in a strange land. But I did have friends I could talk to who understood me— friends who were fun, loving and supportive. The trouble was, they were not in human bodies at the time. There were many of them. I could see them, hear them, and interact with them.

I talked to fairies and had tea parties in my back yard. I talked to little gnomes and woodland creatures and we played games together. The one I called "the little green man" was especially kind and would make me laugh when I was sad.

I even talked to people who had once had bodies, like my grandfather who had died when I was three. He would come to me and talk gently and quietly, and I felt loved and supported. I was always happy when I saw him, and looked forward to his visits. I actually saw him more often after he died than when he was alive. Because no one else saw him, though, I had a lot of one-on-one time that I had not had before.

My favorite conversations, however, were with God. God was a friend to me, and a father figure. (I now realize that the energy had no gender, but my religious background influenced my interpretation.) Every night I'd say my prayers, ask God questions, and ask about experiences in my day. I didn't have to recount anything. God already knew what I'd done and experienced. I told no one about these conversations. I knew instinctively that the relationship was sacred and special—something just for me.

My family thought it was normal for a child to have pretend friends, but when I continued to talk to them when I was five, six, seven…they became frightened. It was the 1950s and I didn't fit the mold. They were especially concerned that I spent so much time with these friends. I preferred these friends to dolls and toys, and even to other people.

Life for me in the world had become almost impossible to master. I tried desperately to act like a normal child, but it wasn't working. I would cling to aspects of my behavior that reaped approval. I became an all-A student, learned to cook and care for my younger siblings, and to dress well. Approval became a substitute for love, but it didn't help the pain of not being loved and known for the person I really was.

At four I was in so much pain that I asked for help. I got it. Help came in the form of an out-of-body being that was large, male, and very aggressive. He quickly learned the ropes of the family, and when I was yelled at, he yelled back. I'll call him Concha, though I didn't think to ask his name at the time. (Four-year-old children don't identify people by name, they identify them by energy and spirit. Even as adults we may not remember a person's name, but we do often remember their energy and spirit.)

So, I let Concha into my body. He took over when I was verbally or emotionally attacked, and he took the stress for me when I was punished and yelled at. He was my savior. He protected me. I didn't know, however, that he harbored many negative traits and was incapable of enlightenment. He was a warrior and took the blows. I would leave, escaping to my out-of-body life. I appreciate his effort even now.

Being out-of-body is like daydreaming. Many people do this, but aren't aware of it. I would suddenly imagine myself with my special friends. We'd be playing on the beach somewhere. They'd talk to me and I'd talk back. I'd laugh and have fun. My parents and friends who were in bodies would ask me who I was talking to—with fear and sometimes anger. I wasn't in control of my body, however. I was "out" with my friends. I'd hear the questions, but I'd also hear Concha grumble, "I'm talking to my friends." He quickly learned that this was not an acceptable response. He'd then respond with, "No one." Later in life, the response would become, "I'm talking to myself."

Being out-of-body had its repercussions. I wasn't facing the pain. I was unable to speak my truth and be myself. The unexpressed words, thoughts, and essence of who I was coalesced into a pain in my stomach. I had trouble eating and was missing school because of it. By eight years old I'd been to many doctors, none of whom could find a problem. I was then taken to a strange kind of doctor. He just talked to me, with my mother in the room. He asked me questions, and although I wanted to, I couldn't answer him truthfully with my mother there. I knew she'd negate my testimonies. I knew this was some kind of test, so I quietly answered with what I felt were the appropriate responses. The doctor then said that he needed to talk to my mother in private, and took me to a room filled with toys. He told me to play with the toys until he and my mother returned.

The room had a very strange energy about it. It was filled with every imaginable toy (none of which interested me), and one wall was entirely mirrored. I felt immediately that something underhanded was going on and that I was being tricked. I picked up a doll and found it boring. I wanted to play with my out-of-body friends, but knew I'd better not. I felt like I was being watched, although I couldn't figure out how. I also knew that if the doctor saw me playing with my out-of-body friends, something very bad would happen to me. I made a decision then to hide all my out-of-body experiences. I began to play with the doll, as a "normal" child might. I'd seen it done enough and had tried to play with friends that way, so I was able to be the perfect actress. The doctor told my mother that he saw nothing wrong with me, so I felt free to escape into my world, but knew I would have to do it in secret. Still, after this experience I definitely felt that there was something wrong with me.

By ten or eleven I realized that my "abnormality" had to be

cured. I decided that my out-of-body friends were part of my "illness" and I told them to leave. From that time on I no longer saw them, but I heard their voices. I was never able, or willing to stop communicating verbally with those who are out-of-body. I still escaped to these conversations and to a life that seemed to be in my head. I functioned reasonably well, but had many problems. I still did not understand how to function in the world with my abilities, and I became confused and depressed. The only people I could talk to about my problems were out-of-body.

When I was twenty-two, I began to journal these conversations. I called this "talking to myself" because I had lost my belief that these people actually existed. I was given advice and directions—some appropriate, some not. I realized that my ego would try to intervene in these conversations, so I learned how to focus on the energy of the speaker and put my own voice and energy aside. These beings did not come into my body. I talked to them and dictated the conversations like an executive assistant taking dictation from a boss.

I had forgotten my conversations with God, and began a journey of searching for God and myself. I studied many esoteric teachings and religions, as well as various forms of natural healing, meditation, yoga, t'ai chi, etc. Through these teachings and practices I re-discovered my true inner self. I honored it, but I didn't bring myself back into body.

Five years ago, after an exciting life of many experiences that included much pain and suffering, I decided to reach for yet another path and began reading about being psychic. I was amazed when reading this book that I actually had all of the abilities mentioned. The book said that if I was serious about psychic study, I'd need a teacher. I didn't know where I'd find one in 1996 in Atlanta, but I told God and the Universe, "I need a psychic teacher."

Two weeks later a friend in pottery class told me that a teacher was coming to town, and he was someone I needed to meet. This teacher taught classes on clairvoyant healing. The teacher was Jim Self, who clarified for me that these beings were real and that the voices were actually different out-of-body beings. He told me that I had been "inhabited" by many beings since the initial intervention by Concha. I had run my body like a person manipulating an electrical car with a joystick.

Since that first meeting with Jim in 1996, many wonderful teachers from the Berkeley Psychic Institute, as well as others from around the country, have helped me to clear the out-of-body beings and energies from my space, enabling me to re-enter my body. These teachers include Ron Ramos, Michael and Raphaelle Tamura, Vessa Reinhart, Jim Self, John Fulton, and Phil Cullinen.

During this time I've also learned about the many levels of out-of-body existence and have begun to spend time with those beings who offer the most light and insight. I have received insight and guidance from Jesus, Archangel Gabriel, Archangel Michael, Jahna the Healing Master, Buddha, and many others. Best of all, I remembered the times when I was a child and would talk with God. I sobbed tears of joy when I first renewed these conversations.

I conversationally check in with God almost daily now. It's difficult to describe the power and depth of this relationship.

Through God I know my source. When I am in touch with my source I know what it is to be invincible, all loving, all knowing. With God I can relax and let go, knowing that the wellspring of life will flow as it must; and with this love and support I have learned to love and trust in myself.

Through this book I am seeking to tap into that wellspring of love and knowledge, and to offer a glimpse of it to others. There is so much wisdom to be gained, and it is all being offered with great love, especially at this time. The words of Gabriel have an energy that's different from the Buddha. The information is spoken in different words and with a different tone and perspective. But the words of the Masters all originate at the same source, and I hope to show that this source is the same in all of us. We are ALL the children of God.

In truth, each of us has the ability to be clairvoyant (clear seeing), clairsentient (clear knowing), and clairaudient (clear hearing). This is an innate ability that comes with Spirit coming into body. The abilities are not apparent to most because belief systems, opinions, attitudes and ego prevent the use of them. Becoming "psychic" does not require the bestowing of a "gift." It is the skill that emerges as one's awareness unfolds.

Awareness is attained by opening one's mind, hearing and sight to new ways of knowing, hearing and seeing. It means that all beliefs, attitudes and behaviors are seen as constructs that we've adapted or developed to exist on this planet. Some of them work quite well to help us adapt to the world. Some of them work for awhile and become outdated. Others were adopted from family or friends and remain unquestioned, such as racial prejudices.

We are entering a new era, and with new beginnings comes a letting go of the past. Many of us are quitting jobs, starting new projects, or moving locations. Others are evaluating relationships and the use of time. Many are moving and moving on, and we are faced with the possible destruction of the known structures and concepts of the life we've known. As time moves forward and we look inside for the answers to create our future, we will find that God exists within us, and that the teachings of all of the angels and Masters are keys to our souls. Our souls are one with God. In time we will honor and exalt those souls and the souls of all.

Although I began recording the messages from the angels and Masters in 1998, I have eliminated the specific dates from this text because the messages are timeless and, in fact, time has no actual meaning. I'm blessed and honored to be a part of this world and this process of unfolding that we are taking together. So begins the documentation of the Masters.

Namasté,
Deborah Hill

A note from God

The Writings of the Masters is not a tool for the many. It is a guide for those who want information about the new millennium and the changes therein. It is not the beginning of a new era of thought. It is the beginning of a new line of communication and understanding of the One. It is time for those who want to know the truth to stand and take their positions. It is now that I ask all of you to stand on your own and begin the ascent into the new consciousness. Take the time to hear the words of others.

For those on this path, there will be little time for rest. It is appropriate to take time to relax and enjoy oneself; but the time it takes to unwind in a detrimental manner (such as heavy drinking and drugs, foul activities and unplanned hostilities) is lost to the world and to yourselves. You then need recovery time. Use your time and energy wisely and you will be rewarded ten-fold.

The Writings *of the* Masters

Part One

Writings Extracted from Dialogues

The spirit of the being known as Jesus

Forgiveness

I have several missions in this particular written work. One is to show how the words of all the prophets intermesh. Another is to relieve the strife that has occurred over the following of my name. A third is to teach the importance of forgiveness; for forgiveness is the spearhead to the heart of the lifelong energy transformation called "enlightenment." The object of our lives here is the enlightenment of the heart and mind through the guidance of the soul. With this, a being can illuminate others and lead them to the God-force.

Forgiveness implies a total acceptance of others. This means accepting that all people have lives they programmed before coming to this planet. The programming will lead them to experiences from which they will learn to become more enlightened. This implies that judgment of others is inappropriate. This does not mean that you should not be aware of the bad habits and negative idiosyncrasies of others. Do not let yourself get in the way of another's negative behavior or experience unless you wish to learn from suffering. There are many who choose the path of suffering. It is not the only path to enlightenment.

Forgiveness does not imply that the person you forgive is beneath you. It is actually an energy transformation. The process in finality is fairly simple. First, you fill yourself with great love emanating from the God-force. Then you allow this energy to pulsate through your heart and energy chakras. This will create an aura of white light. Allow the person you are forgiving to place their "sin" on your aura. Be sure that the aura is of adequate strength before you attempt this. The sin must not penetrate into your inner space. Do not think or feel this sin. Allow your aura to vaporize and metabolize the energy placed there. You may feel a slight twitch of energy, no more than that. Then move on. Think no more of it. It is done.

A person in life may commit a sin several times. Do not let him commit this sin on you. Get out of the way, but forgive him before you go; thus he will learn from the error of his ways. A person must want to be forgiven. Otherwise, he may have chosen a path that involves the pain of others begrudging him. Do not deny him this. Do not forgive someone unless he asks for it. The way to deal with the negative emotions you have is to move on to other people. Let the person go out of your life. Then let the negative energy go, as well.

The spirit of the being known as Jesus

Negative Emotions; Blame

L isten to the true teachings of the Masters, not with the mind of the ego, but with the heart and soul of the true spirit. The mind is a helpful tool. Just as the emotions are not the true heart, the mind is not the true intelligence. Let it rule you and you become empty of heart and soul.

It is true that most crimes are founded on beliefs. For example:

"I believe that this person's opinions are detrimental to humanity."

"I believe that only the men and women of true blood are worthy."

"I believe that bigamists are heathens and are not fit for this earth."

"I believe that I am a poor, unfit soul and deserve to die to put others out of the misery of being with me."

These beliefs are poisonous. They poison the spirit and soul of humanity. Listen to the true heart of the words that are spoken. Learn to listen with your heart and soul, and let the message reach your higher intelligence. This is not as difficult as it sounds. Real knowledge and understanding has a specific tone. It strikes a chord in your heart and in your soul. If you are tense with the belief, if you feel anger or a negative emotion, if you think that you must commit some sin in order to justify your thinking, then you are not thinking with true higher intelligence.

This is not difficult. You hear truths all the time. You know when someone says, "I love you," and means it. You know and can listen for the kindness of others. Start with these simple truths. Listen for them and take them to heart. At the same time, do not take to heart the negativities of others or yourself. Let these ingrained negative ideologies and idiosyncrasies pass. Let the tone of them wither in the wind. Look another way. Certainly do not base your life interpretation on them. It is not our place to judge others. That is the role of the God-force. Our place is to watch, to learn, and to stay positive. This is how we grow. Again, I am not suggesting that you ignore negativity. Just get out of its way. Do not take it to heart. Move away from it and the people broadcasting it.

Saviors are not those who slay in the name of religion. Nor are they professors of holocaust at the expense of the innocent. There has never been a time when I have said, "Mighty are those who know my name." Mighty are those who know their own real names and the source from which they come. Know that you are all powerful in your own right, and that power must be used to further the growth of humanity, not the destruction of it. Destruction of any sort is for God alone. Do not attempt it at any cost.

This does not apply to the destruction of physical property, such as buildings. If the destruction of buildings ruins the lives of other humans, then it is destruction indeed. If it eliminates insufficient housing in order to replace it with pure and more spectacular establishments for the benefit of all, then destruction is not the cause. Look to your heart. Is the aim selfish? If it is, does it harm others? You are not your brother's keeper, nor are you his guardian; but you are responsible for the inadvertent pain you cause in the physical lives of others.

If you destroy another's home, you have hurt him. If you go home because you are tired, and his feelings are hurt because of this, you did not hurt him. You took care of yourself. He hurt himself. If you hit someone and he suffers physical injury, you have hurt him. If you suffer from fatigue and slip, you have hurt yourself. If you leave his abode and he chases after you and is hurt in the process, you did not hurt him.

Let us explore the concept of blame. Blame assumes that one party is superior to the other. There is no such thing. Some of you know and have experienced more than others. This does not make you superior. It just makes you wiser and more experienced. A first grader is not inferior to a senior in high school. He is only younger. You must never blame others for mistakes, just as you cannot blame a two-year-old for trying to get his way by throwing a temper tantrum. You observe and note that he is being manipulative with respect to his behavior, and that he is undergoing a learning process in keeping with his age. Observe your brothers and sisters on this planet as such.

Likewise, you cannot blame others if they must take action that is detrimental to their souls. They will learn the implications of this in due time. You can note if people intentionally hurt you physically or emotionally. You know when they purposefully harm you. Do not blame them, as they are again learning a lesson; but do not let them do this to you again. Get out of the way.

Again, if a person needs to carry out an action that is not to your liking, but is not intentionally done to harm you, do not take offense. You are not responsible for the other person's happiness, and they are not responsible for yours. If a friend has to leave and you want him to stay, let him go. Allow others to take care of themselves. That is our number one function while on Earth. We are given bodies and souls in them, and must do what is best for us. Never blame someone for doing this.

Now listen to this minute but significant difference. If a person purposefully puts himself in situations that inadvertently hurt others, he is committing a sin. For example, if Joe asks Susan to a dance on a night when he knows he will be too tired to attend, he is setting the situation up for pain. If he continually makes commitments when he knows he won't be able to carry them out, he is causing pain. This is his responsibility. Take others into account when you make your plans. Do not suffer from commitments, but do not intentionally set yourself up for plans you know you should not keep.

The spirit of the being known as Jesus

Illumination

L et us begin with a story about my past in Jerusalem. There seems to be much speculation and great stories about my youth. In reality, it was very similar to any child's at that time. It was a great time of transformation. The Romans were making great and sweeping changes in the land, and the people were in flux. Some were confused by the ways of these Romans and were unable to adjust. The soldiers thought of these people as dissenters. In actuality they were just ignorant or slow. We were desert people after all, and although the culture was far advanced spiritually, there were many areas in which we were not adept.

It was at this time when the God-force determined that a shock in the time-space continuum should be felt by the people of this area to shake them out of their ignorance. A shock in the time-space continuum occurs when a being of greater intelligence or more experience from other realms enters into the world and creates an opportunity for growth. I was just one of the many who were sent down at this time to shake the foundations of the present-day thinking.

Many were silent observers. I was lead to speak after my Bar Mitzvah, in my thirteenth year. I was told in my heart that I was to point out a few of the idiosyncrasies of the religion, and how they could serve a higher purpose if altered. I was initially appalled to be having such thoughts. I had no wish to shake the foundations of my religion and the culture of my homeland, but the need to speak was in me. I was torn for about a year, saying a few things here and there to people who were close to me. My mother and father were tolerant and sympathetic, but were unable to refute my messages. Slowly the words I said began to spread. Soon others with whom I was not so familiar began to question me. I had to tell the truth, as you know. Beings based in other spiritual realms are unable to lie. I told the people what I saw.

Soon I found strength in the truth, though it often brought conflict from others. I did not want to lie and I was not of a temperament to cause problems, but problems occurred. The climate around us became vicious and we had to leave Bethlehem.

I am telling you this not to tell you my history, but to tell you that many children feel as I did. They know the truth, but are afraid or unwilling to voice what they know because of the repercussions of their words. It is time for the adults of the world to look to the children for the truth. If you trust in them, they will not lie. You will know it if they do. Just as you know love when it is given you, you know untruth when it is told to you. Trust your feelings. Do not trust your mind. Your mind is a tool, not a seer. Remember your Higher Mind is based on the wisdom of the heart and soul, interpreted through the intellectual energy of experience.

Most people are not driven to God as I was. I lived and breathed the God-force in my being. I could not turn away, and did not wish to if I could. It was always clear that I would serve the Higher Source no matter the implications or punishment I took. There was no question. Many of you on the planet now feel this resolve.

Now let us move on to another topic. I want to discuss the process of illumination. Illumination is not an instantaneous flash of knowing. Seeing something for the first time might give one the impression that he has moved to another level of reality. Seeing the truth always has this effect. This does not imply a shift in consciousness, however. Many people have had experiences and consider themselves enlightened after this. The experience can range from tripping over a log on the beach to a near-death episode. Many books and parables are written about the latter, and this leads others to desire the same. The belief is that one is not enlightened unless he has such an experience. This is unfortunate.

Enlightenment does not come from one illumination. Enlightenment is a process of several lifetimes, which leads to a greater understanding. As you grow, so does the eternal consciousness. You can not expect that the eternal consciousness will leap because you bump into a log; but your ever-present vigilance and dedication to the continuing understanding of this illumination by way of the log will lead to a greater understanding. This understanding will permeate the consciousness of the One. Many such experiences of many, or some very powerful experiences of a few, will alter the level of understanding of all humanity. Whether these experiences are simple or powerful, they will alter the level of understanding of all humanity. Seek illumination if this heightens your awareness of the God-force and the path you are on. Do not base your understanding of the workings of the One on the number or presence of illuminations in your life. You can choose to go on a roller coaster and experience a great thrill. This does not mean that you are more understanding of the emotion of fear than is someone who has not experienced the ride.

There is something that I would like to pass on. It was during the time of the resurrection when I first became aware of a strange sensation called "white heat." It illuminated through me until I thought it would rip my soul to shreds. I felt that it was the light of the Lord passing through me. I now understand that I may have wanted to experience such an illumination to justify or verify the experiences I was having. One is not often crucified, and I wanted to experience verification from the Lord that I had acted correctly. It was not inappropriate to ask such a thing, but this light did not indicate more understanding on my part. Experiences of illumination are like beacons of light along the path to verify that you are on the correct path. Some people do not need these. Some need to trust that God exists without seeing visible evidence. When this trust is present, the illuminating experiences may occur. Trust in yourself. That is the true beacon of God's understanding.

This is a lengthy topic and I could give many examples; however, I will give only a few. Last year a woman from Conyers said she saw the Mother Mary. Many flocked to her door and prayed for this miracle to occur. All of the people who wanted illumination experienced the vision of the Mother Mary. Those who did not want or believe this did not see it. This does not mean that those who saw were more "awakened." In fact, there were many who felt this was blasphemy and that the truth of Mary is in the knowing in the soul. This is also true. It does not matter. If this "sight" lead some to seek the truth, it was beneficial.

Another experience happened in Tokyo several years ago. A volcano of tremendous proportions exploded. The power and force of this explosion was enough to put the fear of God into many atheists. Again, this served a purpose. I do not suggest that God is to be feared. Fear him only in the face of your own frailties, for only you can bring forth the wrath of God onto yourself. This volcano killed many, but it also brought God into the hearts of millions. It was transformative. It was an experience of illumination, not enlightenment.

A few years ago a man jumped from a building in order to commit suicide, but he landed in a large pile of refuse. God gave him the opportunity to see that life extends beyond the known realm. This man lives today and thinks he is a prophet because God gave him this insight. The man is not enlightened, but his experience does serve a purpose.

Several weeks later he confronted another man, a businessman, in an elevator and told him about his experience. Coming from such a direct source, the businessman could not refute the story. He saw the truth coming from this man. The businessman experienced an illumination and is now more firmly on the path to understanding.

Isn't it all so amusing and delightful? Don't you just want to go out and experience more? Every experience you have is an illumination in its own right. Do not underestimate the power of your everyday experiences. They are the lifeblood of the One. You are very important to the continuance of the eternal force. Your every move is noted and affects all of those around you. If the moves you make do not appear to light up, be comforted in knowing that no one is separate or apart from all that is. You are on your path if you wake up each day with the knowledge that you are seeking truth and understanding. That is all there is. Be happy with yourself and your life. That is the greatest of all illuminations, and in time, will lead you closer to true enlightenment.

The spirit of the being known as Jesus

Illumination; Education; Love

I want to discuss the process of illumination as it relates to education. The educational systems of many countries are lacking in the factor of illumination. Children are taught to learn through the mind—to experience life intellectually. The brain is honed until it can conquer the soul and heart. The emotions are squelched and hidden in the face of reason. It is then felt that mankind can make its way in the world by leading with the head.

Children would learn so much more if they were illuminated with knowledge. When they see something in this way, they remember it always. They remember not only the fact or lesson, but the excitement and beauty of the experience, as well.

In ancient times it was common practice to use this illuminative factor in teaching. Children were lead to the answer and then left to continue the journey on their own. When the answer was finally hit upon, the child was overjoyed by the discovery and understanding. The joy of illumination and the power of the lesson had an impact that would prevail through many more trials of higher learning. This quest for knowledge was then taken on as a gift and not an ordeal.

Teach your children with illumination. Do not attempt to drum information into them. Teach them to discover the truth for themselves.

Let us use the example of history. Instead of naming dates and events, have the children play the parts of characters they wish to learn about. They will have to study the times and the characterizations, the customs and the past customs. Attitude and attire will have to be learned. While undergoing this process of study, the child is more apt to pick up the actual spirit of the times. So now the knowledge begins to blossom into an understanding of the age.

Certainly one cannot act out all of history in one semester; but a few plays, a poem or two, or a short story will teach the mind a pattern of understanding through seeing the whole picture. From there the mind can expand its power of imagination to encompass the other aspects of history, as well.

Another example would be learning to read and write. These two must come together. In order to write, one must read. All knowledge and creativity is built upon the knowledge and creativity of the past. We are all stepping on the shoulders of our forefathers. Read and think—then write. Read in a pleasant wooded park, feeling the breeze and sun on your body. Let the reading emote feelings in you. Let your creativity soar from your reading. Then let this creativity blend into your hand and sweep onto the page in a wonderland of words. This is true writing.

Teachers must learn to understand the difference between resistance to learning and being unable to learn. The former is laziness and a barrier to be overcome. The latter is a sign that the student is not meant to go in that direction. Find the topic that is enjoyable and of greatest benefit to this particular person, and let him move on his own path. Then you can guide him on to new areas in keeping with his growth.

Likewise, if a child shows an extreme aptitude in one subject, but prefers another, let her explore her preference. The child may have been a great scientist in a past life, but has come into this life to explore art and creativity. Forcing her into a scientific career would prevent her from living out her lifelong goal.

A child cannot be too immersed or engrossed in a topic. It is like eating sweets. Serve a person all of the sweets he wants and he will soon tire of them. Allow a child to pursue his interests wholeheartedly and he will either move on to something else, or he may become the next Einstein in his field of choice. Children are much wiser than many of us realize. They know where they are headed more than most of us, and if given some semblance of freedom, they will go there.

Discipline is necessary in the following areas: cleanliness, tidiness, timeliness, responsibility to others and oneself, taking care of one's body with healthy eating, exercise and sleep, and staying tuned in to God and his messages to you through prayer or meditation. These things must be structured for a child in order for him to ground himself on this planet. With this structure in place, he will be free to explore his world and his longings for information and experiences.

It is getting late now and before I leave, I want to mention a few words on love. Love as it is ordinarily known is shackled in the confines of the base emotions and bodily hormones. We intertwine love with our lessons and think that love will find its way through the murk. Do not expect love to emerge from your turmoil. Do not look to love to heal you from your strife. Instead, let love be in your heart at all times, no matter the circumstance or the trial. There it will serve its full function, giving strength and light to you and those around you.

Love is not a reward, nor is it a gift. It is not a tool to be used to gain acceptance. Love is not a game to be played in order to have your life fulfilled. Love is an energy force that has no form and no intention. Love is like sunlight as it shifts through the clouds and then over mountains. Love is like sunlight on a rainy day when the clouds hide it. Love is a force that is an essential part of our universe. It is not to be owned or identified, or placed on a person or thing. Allow love to permeate you at all times. Allow yourself to bask in the energy, no matter the elements surrounding your life at the time. Let the light of love surround you and move through you as a heat wave on a cold day. Love is not something to be earned; it is ever present. Just open to it and it will heal you and allow you to heal others with its radiance. Just open to it and see for yourself what happens.

Do not look for love; know it's there. Work your way through the darkness in your soul until you feel its warmth. The barriers you experience are your own. Blast them with all your might and continue to blast them again until you see the light of love. Then the light at the end of the tunnel will inspire you to open even more. Do not be afraid of pain. Pain occurs when you are closed to love. Pain occurs when you close yourself because of a lack of the expectation of it. Love is curtailed when you feel snubbed or rejected. You think pain is the opposite of love, so you close yourself off. The pain is not the other side of love; it is the closing off to it. Pain of the heart is the lack of love. The resistance to it comes from you. There is only one way out of the pain—open yourself to love.

The spirit of the being known as Jesus

Adjusting to Guidance from the Masters

In this section I will discuss who the Masters are. They are varied and from different times of life. Some have traveled great distances from other realms. Others have lived one life on Earth and moved on. Some of their names are Buddha, Krishna, Baba Rama, Mohammed, Krishna Mufti, The Great Walhalla, Sevananda Malaya, Brevatan, Onaya, Malaya ha Leah, Moses, Judah, Abraham, Joseph, Mary . . . I could go on. Still this is a good start. You have heard of some of these, others are less well known. Some have been on this planet for millennia, but are discreet in their ways. Others have "made a name" for themselves. No matter, they all have much to say and will be glad to speak to you. Talk to them first in meditation to get to know them.

Let's move on to another topic. It was important that I not allow others to look into my past as a man on Earth because they would have used this past to dissect my character. My youth was filled with growth experiences, just as any on this planet. I did not want to be judged. I did not want others to interpret my words through my character. The healing and energy I portrayed to others was proof in itself. I did not want those around me to search my past for proof of the truth.

Now I feel people can handle the information I give them in a new context. Now we can move to a new level of understanding and use the lessons of my upbringing for growth of others.

Too often humans get caught up in the day-to-day affairs of their lives. They want to strain all information through this sieve of the mind. This taints the information and allows it to take on a new character and tone. The truth is diluted in the mire of the human mindfulness; translucent in its entirety, but transparent in pieces. The essence of the truth is often misrepresented by the characters who portray it. The personality of the few who hear, or listen, is diffused into the message and becomes tainted.

Take the time to remember all of the stages of learning that have occurred in your life—all of the stages you've gone through. They were like stepping stones in your growth and understanding. It is through your experiences that you learn to know the truth for yourself. You learn to see the world through your own REAL eyes and then act. This is when you begin to take responsibility for your own actions and errors—and you continue on your journey.

The truth is fragmented throughout the globe. Look at the individual facets and allow them to lead you to the whole. Talk to God everyday. You will be heard.

The spirit of the being known as Jesus

Emotions

First of all, I want to note that we don't want people to argue whether these words come from Jesus or Buddha or Allah. The point of the book is to tell the Truth. You know that the words come essentially from the same source. We are all God's children. We are all of the same heart and mind. We all communicate with ourselves in the same manner. We are no different in spirit or in essence. We are all on the same path and the path leads to and begins with the same God-force. You know this. Allow it to unfold and do not allow anyone to argue with the true source or the identity of its writers. It is irrelevant. The true source of all knowledge, truth, and awakening is the One. Now I will move on to another subject.

When the heart is hurting, the emotions begin to shut down. They tire with too much activity. That is why people commit suicide after prolonged depression. The emotions deplete them of so much fuel that they have nowhere to turn but to death.

People do not always ask for help because positive guidance seeking is not an act of the emotions. It is either a logical response or a desire of the soul. When depressed, a person cannot see the soul, and the mind is too weak to have any real power.

It may seem that positive emotions give energy, but they do not give fuel. Positive emotions and negative emotions both rely on the use of energy. It is their effects that differ. Positive emotions open the way for a person to see the true heart and soul. It is here that one receives energy. Negative emotions cut us off from our soul.

Several methods are effective in transforming negative emotions to positive:

1. Don't go there. Just stop the negativity.
2. Pretend that you are feeling some other way; or even try to be someone else for a few moments.
3. Try using the intellect to a great extent. Read a particularly taxing or challenging book. Try to understand a new idea.
4. Go to sleep. Negative emotions are often fueled by lack of physical energy. You might try eating something healthy—not something sweet.
5. Smile.
6. Call a friend for a few words of encouragement or for a joke. Call a friend who can snap you out of it. Don't call to "let a load off your back." Do not burden your friends so. Take only a short amount of time and don't drain them. A true friend will also gain energy by cheering you up and helping you move to a new level.
7. Call on me if the above doesn't work.

Let's look at how the emotions work in life. You use them to fuel the imagination, which helps you to develop new avenues of creativity. The emotions serve as the ballast and the charge, or spice, that you need to move into new areas of activity. It would be difficult to try new things if there was no emotional involvement. It would be especially difficult to meet new people, make new friends who teach you, learn new concepts, etc. The emotions are the fuel for creation. The tools for creation come from the mind and soul.

The body is also involved in creating with emotional inspiration. Many athletes have great emotional drive. Good actors and actresses have very deep emotions. Artists, musicians, and scientists of vast proportion all use their emotions to charge their activities; however, scientists do not always display these emotions. They channel them directly to the mind. A scientist may become excited by a new idea or concept, or by a new design or discovery. This excitement and drive of discovery is emotional in nature.

Emotions are prevalent in nature. Animals live with emotions. They use them to travel to vast territories. Like fuel, the emotions drive hummingbirds across the ocean as much as the food they've stored. Watch a cat when it attacks. Watch a bird as it catches its prey. There is an emotional charge in the activities of animals. Of course, pets are very emotionally bound to their masters. Look at animals closely and you will see that the emotions rule as much as the physical body. The intellect, of course, is very basic. It is based upon bodily functions. Animals cannot reason. Do not try to communicate with them, even in pictures, by showing them the implications of actions. The animal mind cannot follow a sequence of thoughts. They cannot see that a certain activity causes a reaction. The body of an animal learns through its senses and impulses to act. Pain and inefficiency are great teachers for the body.

Enjoy positive emotions. See how a smile adds life to your body and hands. Too much concentration will deplete you. The intellectual mind will use the emotional energy to concentrate. This is exhausting. The mind is like a wheel that turns incessantly in circles. It will always return to the same position unless forced into new thought. New thoughts are very rare. The mind likes to mull over the same concept. When the electrical activity that fuels thought occurs, it uses energy. Patterns are formed, as are reactions in the body. These patterns take up energy. In order to break these patterns one must try to think of different thoughts. Once begun, it isn't difficult.

Imagine a story about someone you know. This has emotional charge, but will help fuel the mind to move in another direction. Try to solve a math problem or crossword puzzle. Remember the names of your first grade class. Any type of nontraditional thought will free up energy. This energy will then be available for use on other topics, or for your own fueling of the soul.

Some people release their fears with therapy. Others try cognitive reasoning to retrain the brain. Whatever works is fine. It is important that the therapy not become the focus of the treatment. The aim is to be healed, or released, from these negative patterns. The aim is for a person to release the bonds of the mental activities and emotional traumas. The confusion occurs when the trials of therapy become the aim and not the outcome of freedom. Do not make therapy a hobby. Learn and move on. Also, do not think that the same therapy will work in all cases. Different types of thought blockages require different blasts of dynamite. Sometimes a hug is all that's needed to release someone from a lifelong habit of feeling unloved. Try it sometime. It will also heal the person giving the hug. All true healers become healed in the process.

The spirit of the being known as Buddha

The Search for Truth

I am the spirit of the man they called Buddha. I am happy to be able to communicate with the many souls who would like information from the Masters. I have not had this opportunity for many years.

There was a time when I was lost and afraid. I went on a long search for the truth, believing that there was no hope for life. I felt that all of us would die or hang in the throws of disparity. I was not aware of the true purpose of the everlasting light. I thought we were meant to be perfect when we came to Earth. It is not true. We are ever changing and far from perfecting the total truth. We emerged out of the eternal womb as flowers of light. Far from our homes we were swept up by the Holy Spirit into a new area of awareness—the soul.

It is best to relate to the world as a child—with innocent eyes we must face the world, never with judgment or pain. Release the pain and judge only yourself. For all else is illusion.

If you see something you don't like, you don't understand it. This is not a new concept. Then again, very few of them are. We are constantly rebuilding ourselves with the ideas of old.

24

Each time we hear them, we see them in a new light, which then shapes us to become more of who we are and less of what we thought we knew. This sounds like a riddle, but taken apart, it is truth.

Stand tall in the remnants of truth. For what you don't understand will surely come back around and you will then be able to pick up the pieces. Do not be tempted to take parts of a truth and paste them together. This is false truth and leads to failure and lack of growth. If there are holes in your thinking, leave them there. In time, they will fill in. If you must, surround the confusion with gold light in order to pay it some attention. Confusion begs for attention. It has no patience for the time it takes to solve the equations. But life is a never-ending riddle with no pat answers, or questions for that matter.

Leave this alone for now. Let's get back to our previous discussion of equations and nonsense. I was saying that I was alone and afraid. Have you noticed that it is impossible to be alone unless you're afraid, or vice versa? If you are afraid, you are forgetting that you are never alone; and if you feel alone, you SHOULD feel afraid, because you have forgotten that you are a part of the eternal. Feel afraid; so afraid that you turn back to God. Ah, every thing and feeling has its purpose, eh?

Is it not simple to realize that ALL of life is real? We learn as much from our play as we do from our "serious" talk—maybe more. We remember the humor after the words are gone. "When you're smiling, the whole world smiles with you." It's true you know—on many planes. Ah, I digress.

Let me continue the story of how difficult my life was when I thought about how difficult life was. I could really settle into the mire and waste away; but I stopped. You know how? The mire is a dead end. You can stay in it only so long and any living person will get terribly bored. Why do you think people kill themselves from depression? There is nowhere else to go if you don't want to get out of the murk. So I said one day, "Now what? I can't just sit here. There must be another way. There must be something I'm not getting here."

All of a sudden I looked up and a beam of light flashed into my cave. Riding on the beam of light was a crow. The crow flew by my side and began pecking at the ground. Brought in like an angel, it just went about its business as if nothing had happened. The crow knew the miracle of life existed in every moment. The crow did not call attention to itself. It just existed in every moment in the knowing Oneness of existence. The everyday moments of its life were not extraordinary. All of the moments of life are extraordinary and so none of them are out of the ordinary. Life itself is an ever-present miracle.

So why do we forget this? We forget this and even make up moments to remember so we can then say we saw a miracle and believe. We don't realize that we live in the miracle always. Do not attempt to make some moments more spectacular than others. All moments are precious and all are special in their own way. The growth-producing and unpleasant ones are the more trying; but the happy are even more difficult in their own way because we are tempted to forget the Almighty when we are happy. Make the effort to see that all of life is one continuum; that all of life is a miracle from the time of existence, and live each "ordinary" moment as if it were just that—a moment in the continuum of all existence. Then each moment is precious and each moment is the same, only different in its tone and integrity.

We are not unusual or different from each other. We are all different parts or moments on the continuum of the gene pool. The gene pool has remained in existence after millions of years; but now we are trying to say that some are better than, or different from others. There is no difference between us. We are all a part of the same continuum. One part lights up here, another there. It is all the same thing. Would you say that your liver is superior to your brain? No. You cannot live without a liver or without a brain. So how can we judge different parts of the eternal body? One man may seem out of place, but he is just a different part of the whole. He serves a different function that we don't understand—and don't need to understand for the time being.

So now we see that we are just simple particles in the molecular structure of the planet; that each day of our lives is part of a greater whole; that we are merely simpletons on the cosmic scale; and each day is miraculous. What do we do with this? Where can we go from here? The next step is to notice that you ARE here. You have this opportunity to experience those days and to act in them. Use them to their fullest potential. Do not waste your precious miracle days by thinking about something else. Be like the crow that flies in on a sunbeam and then goes about his business. Go about your business knowing that you, too, flew in on a sunbeam of the eternal, and will forever be a part of the greater miraculous whole.

The spirit of the being known as Lao Tsu

A Clear Mind

The key to the heart is a clear mind. There is so much rigma-role in the world, with thoughts flying every which way. It is essential that the mind is clear, like a crystal blue ball of coral awaiting your command. Expand the mind to fill every cavity in and beyond your head. It is then that the soul can fill it with questions and observations of the truth. The truth is free for those with a clear mind. Did I say clear? Can I say it enough? I seem stern in this respect. I am stern. It is the only key that will turn the inner soul to the truth.

For example, tonight the Tibetan monks performed in a very large church in Atlanta, with impressive acoustics. The people in the room were listening to the Tibetan monks sing to eterni-ty. The spirits of the people were enraptured with the feel of the tunes and the places they were taken. The effect was miraculous and powerful, and all were enlightened for the time being. It was a mass healing in vast proportion with everyone in the room experiencing inner freedom and outer light. Peace reigned and for once, the negativity was numbed, but there was very little understanding.

It is important that people see and think clearly. Let the bells of higher thought resonate through the minds of the few. That is our only hope—to get the people started on the planet and to lead them to see the truth.

Like the wind that blows through the fields and valleys of the Himalayas, there is an essential energy that blows through the minds of all who are present on Earth. The wind has a message, and the message is, "Be still and hear the wind." Let the wind blow through you and clear your mind of all thoughts. Let the sparks of the newly found void then spring questions to life. There you will find the answers, as well, and the truth will resound. Know the power of the empty mind.

When your mind is clear, you feel as if the windows were suddenly cleaned and you can see how bright it is. And what is inside your head? What thoughts are you thinking? Nothing and none. You are an ever-present being looking out from a vast horizon of space. The power of the mind is vast and the depth of it is even more inspiring. The mind seeks to orient us with thoughts. With these we seem to balance ourselves on the planet. Our thoughts create the illusion of consistency. We think the same thing or have the same reaction, and suddenly we feel there is a strong footing. We know this path. We've taken it many times before. It is familiar and we feel comfortable on it. The next instant we think we are the thought pattern and we are lost. We become the repetition and the thought is now us. Gone. We are gone. Nothing left of Higher Mind. Nothing left of us. Phwet.

You can be sitting and meditating, or thinking about something important. Then the one thought becomes another, and another sentence follows. The thought turns into a story and the story into a dream. You are lost. Gone. Phwet. Out of here.

You ask for forgiveness and clear your mind. Then a pretty woman or man passes through and you are observing. The observation turns to desire. The desirous urge becomes desirous thought. The thoughts keep growing until you are with the person in your head. The two of you travel together on this imaginary journey. You are gone. Phwet. Out of here.

Someday, you say, you will clear your head for good. Then you begin to think about how that day will be. You are gone.

So the next day you feel you should pay attention to an activity. In order to take your mind off of itself, you focus on a task—one nail into wood, two nails. You think about how the piece will look; how it will feel to sit in this chair knowing you made it; how proud you are of yourself for making it. You are gone.

You think your empty mind is boring? No. Your life is boring. If your mind has nothing to observe but your endless nothingness, it will be bored. Read something. Write something. Take a walk and look around you. Call a friend. Start a project that takes concentration and real thought. Do something that you like, or do nothing if you like. Just do something that works for you with an empty mind.

Once you have steadied the mind, you can take journeys with it. You can travel to a different land, send thoughts to relatives and friends, figure out a way to change the oil in your car, or solve a puzzle that has been nagging at you. There are many things you can do with the mind once it is quiet and controlled. The difference here is that the mind is under your control. You are not under the control of the mind. The mind is not rambling. You are behind the wheel, steering it.

Focused meditative thinking is one of the most powerful tools for getting something done. There was once a woman who interacted with a tree. The woman later thought about the tree and knew it needed some care. So she sent healing energy out to the tree. She consciously thought about the last time they were together and she felt the energy of the tree. She then sent it some healing energy with her mind, and it worked. Guided meditative thought is a very powerful healer, indeed.

Clear, directed thought can often seem abrupt. Like a cool wind moving off an iceberg, a clear thought gathers no unnecessary air particles. In order for it to register well in the other person's mind, you must insert a little heart. Some insert more than others do. When you open your heart, your crystalline blue thoughts will carry a little warmth with jewel-like clarity. This will make them more palatable to others. However, negative thoughts—even well meaning negative thoughts—need to be buried and never displayed.

The spirit of the being known as Lao Tsu

Moving Through Your Day

Like a cool wind, the mind flows through the crevices of life. Looking through eyes of glass you see the crystalline forces of the Almighty at work. There is nothing to fear when the mind is calm. All is clear and in sight. The actions necessary are apparent and clearly defined. You can do no wrong; only move as appropriately noted.

Let us look at the concept of the warrior. A true warrior is clear-minded, strongly focused, compassionate, open-hearted and committed to serving the goals of the Almighty at any cost. Let us take this further. The analogy to a warrior in life is a good one. Let us look at how the warrior operates.

Warriors of the Almighty are sure-footed and strong-willed. They are ever present and focused on the task ahead, yet at all times remain aware of the events and beings surrounding them. They are never far from the center of their being, nor are they far from the core they call home. There is a need to keep moving through life and acting in the name of the Almighty.

This seems a life of stark realities and deep truths—not

much fun. In truth, the way of the Almighty is a way of light and happiness. The Almighty does not want us to suffer. Suffering comes when we get off course. When in step with God's Will, you will find that your path is sure-footed and light-hearted. There is nothing so joyful as being aware and on the path.

Take a series of incidents in your life. You wake up in the morning and have a cup of tea. You look about you and see your surroundings. You focus on your body and attend to it. You feed it, bathe it, and exercise it. These are important functions to perform.

Now you may see that your mind is cloudy. So you sit and clear it through meditation or some other form that suits you, such as prayer or meditational readings. When the mind is attended to as the body is, you are ready to begin your day in strength and clarity.

Next you pay attention in all of your senses to what is occurring in your reality that day. Where are you going? You may use a calendar, but if you pay attention, you will know ahead of time if the people you've committed to will keep the appointments. The secretary may have written the appointment down, but the client is ill or has another meeting. You can sense this before the call comes from the secretary to cancel. So, you take what you have in front of you and see where your path truly lies for the day.

Sit in your chair and move assuredly through the tasks you feel you need to accomplish. If you have a feeling of dread, you may be working in the wrong area; or you may have some internal resistance to the task, which prevents proper service. Look at what you are feeling. Try to release the feeling. If it remains, look at where it originates. What would your life be like if you did not do the task you dread? Would you be happier?

Do what feels correct in your day. Feel the energies that pass through you. See where the day leads you and act in each moment as you feel you must. You may have a task in front of you that you dread. After examining your thoughts and feelings, you see no internal strife or issues preventing you from performing the task. But the dread remains. Turn to another project that flows more easily. You may find that the original project was being done prematurely. New data may come about; or the entire project may be cancelled because of outlying complications of which you were unaware. There is rarely a time to force yourself to perform tasks that are dreadful. Move in the path of least resistance.

Laziness is not an obstacle to be honored, however. It's not appropriate to play when you're meant to work. Play would not be fulfilling at this time if there is a project to be done. You may want to call someone on the phone to chat. There is a time for social interactions; however, if there is a task to be done, the conversation will turn sour.

How do you know when you are acting appropriately? Actions create energy. If you feel positive energy around you as you create or perform a task, you are acting appropriately. If you feel tired and sluggish, or if you dread what you're doing and look at the clock continuously, you are not on the correct path. If you do this every day of your life, you are not living the destiny you were meant to live. When you're on the correct path, you will feel light and positive. Your way will light up before you and you will feel self-assured and grateful. If you do not feel these things, wake up and look around. Try to do only those things that make you feel this way.

If you have a job you love and have a bad day, you may chalk it up to a learning time. However, if you dread going to work, and hate the projects you work on, you are not on your path.

If you look around you and dislike the people you are with, you are in the wrong place. Do not blame the others or try to change them. No one else feels as you do. You are an outcast in that setting because you don't belong there. Find where you are comfortable and worthwhile. When you are in the correct group, your input will help the others and you will be grateful for their company.

Again, you may have a bad day or a bad week. The sun may be in a distant sign and your mercury is off. You may have a slight touch of the flu, which is influencing how you think and perform. This happens. Acknowledge it and move on. Many unexplained things occur in life. The mind cannot grasp the importance or the meaning behind them.

You may wonder if you are here for the purpose of helping humanity or for helping yourself. There is no difference. The principles I've discussed apply to the act of giving, as well. When you want to give of yourself, it feels good to do for others; but when you are tired and afraid, depressed or unfit in any other way, your giving is done because you need to be fed. Feed yourself at these times. When you are alone and afraid, you are not in your true element. You need time to return to your home. You need to refuel in order to serve. The fact that you are on this planet attests to your desire to fulfill your own need for growth, with the understanding that you are a part of the greater whole.

Greater service to humanity occurs when you must say what you know. This process is inevitable when you reach a certain point in your evolution. You must speak. It is a natural occurrence and does not take great sacrifice. It occurs as easily as eating or sleeping. The need to reveal the truth becomes the sole focus of your life when you reach a certain level of understanding. That is the necessary order. What happens after that? I don't know.

There are other planetary systems and places you can go to renew your journey toward growth. That is a possibility when you reach a certain level; when you have released all the knowledge within you and have let go of your holds on the beings in the gene pool; when you have let go of your friends in the spiritual plane, and your allies on the Earth; when you have released your fears of unknown worlds and have seen only the truth for many years. Then you are ready to leave this galaxy if you so desire. That may be awhile for most of us. Still, transitory visits are possible.

In the astral plane you can move into a different realm. You may explore other beings and systems. These dreams take on a different light. They appear strange and it is hard to remember them because there is nothing to relate them to here on the earth plane.

There is much you can do on the astral plane once you are bored here. You can travel to any number of realms and meet with beings if you so desire. They may have lessons to teach, or they may be so foreign that there is nothing to share. This form of travel is like thought gone into the ethers.

The spirit of the being known as Lao Tsu

Judgment; Lessons; Attack

You may or may not realize that there are obstacles in your head that seem a part of you. You honor them because they seem to serve a purpose. You take them for granted and accept that they are one of the finer points of life. Take rational judgment, for example. You see a person who is unkind. You then believe you are superior and are able to judge this person. You build a whole life around avoiding unkind people. Every time you see someone who seems unkind you set up your stand. You stand behind your beliefs, pointing in your head and sometimes chatting about this judgment to others. You feel justified in this behavior because you have recognized this "bad" behavior and you are "stomping" it out.

Take a look at yourself. You are being unkind. What you have identified, you have become. What you see, you are. This self-perpetuating behavior based upon what you see is quite common and is the main way that people become stuck in their beliefs about others.

So what do you do? You see someone who is being unkind.

Look further. You then see someone who is hurt and angry. Look further. Do not shy away. It is difficult to look this closely. You see the pain. You see the journey the person has taken. Then you are inside of their world—and their world is painful. We will talk about dealing with the pain in a moment. If you do not put up a barrier of judgment, you will begin to see that this is a being who has been on a journey and is finding his/her way in the world. You may be able to help, if the person wants your help. You may just see something in his/her journey that teaches you something about your own journey. Nonetheless, you are not in judgment. What you see is merely another being on the path—like you.

How do you deal with your pain? Sometimes you live through it. Sometimes you laugh at it. Other times you sit and stare at it and wither away into depression. None of these are particularly more or less effective.

How about if you just drop it? Don't look at it more than is necessary. Move on to the next topic. Note the pain, catalogue it, and move on. Do not let your mind take over and tell your heart to react. Do not let your mind tell you that you must process this pain. Do not even think that by feeling someone else's pain you will understand him better. You will not. Instead you will be stuck in the pain just as he is. Move out of it by letting it go. Let it go. Let it go. Don't even hold it for a moment. Remember the game called Hot Potato? If someone throws you a hot potato, let it go lest you get burned. Don't try to set it somewhere. Don't try to save the potato. It's poison to you. Nix it.

It's difficult to look at a person going through a period of lessons in life. You see yourself in this same position and you don't want to look. Look at it harder. Lessons are a good thing. Let the people you are observing have the blessing of a safe journey. Let them know you honor their journey by giving them the respect of notice. You do not have to go to where they are. Just acknowledge and honor them on their path. If a person's actions are harmful to you or threatening in a real, physical sense, then all of the above is forgotten. Get out of the way. Leave the person. Do not judge. Do not look. Leave and let it all go before it sticks to you. Negativity breeds negativity. It is like a virus that spreads rapidly and assuredly. It will grab you by the throat. Look away quickly before you are stuck. When attacked, don't try to fight with the person. Run. Don't try to defend yourself. Deflect and run. Don't even try to cheer him/her up. You can't. Smile, bow, and run like the wind. Take time each day to clean out your energy field of leftover negativity.

The spirit of the being known as Jesus

Living in the Moment; Enlightenment

There comes a time in people's lives when they realize they must choose between living life on a day-to-day basis and the need to succeed materially. There is no other reason to choose life, so they choose to succeed. This is all-important in the scheme of things.

When you choose to live life moment by moment, you choose the optimal course for the soul. When you choose material success as a life goal, you only see yourself on a path. The path may be narrow or wide, difficult or adventurous, painful or joyful. The path you choose depends on the lessons you choose to learn from, and the attitude you desire when learning them.

When you to live moment by moment you live each day as it comes, without a path or a destination. This is extremely difficult to do. People traditionally need a goal to move them forward. They need to feel that their efforts will be rewarded, and that the results of living on their path will be fame, fortune, stature, pride, knowledge, or best of all, love. This is the dream.

It is felt that the purpose of man's existence is to get one chance at succeeding. Women or men may take careers, or take on a hobby, or raise children. Whatever the goal, the acknowledgement of it by others is of utmost importance to them.

The need to feel loved and appreciated is a universal need based upon the need to succeed. When you have no goal but to live life as it is meant each day, you have no need for appreciation because you know that you did what needed to be done in the moment. With this correctness of action comes a true sense of self-worth, which needs no fulfillment from others. When you live your life on the path of day-to-day existence, you live the life you are meant to live.

It is assumed that a day-to-day existence is a life without accomplishments. This is not the case. When you live each day in awareness of what you must do, and in happiness of its fulfillment, you accomplish more than you can imagine. The actions will flow out of you and you will produce beyond your wildest dreams. Your art or trade will flow because the creative energy has no limitations of purpose. You will fend for yourself in the financial sphere because you will know in each moment what you must do; and your actions will mirror your inner understanding of the signs and signals of life. This is the true path.

There is no truth in tying yourself to one path like a dog on a chain attached to a moving sidewalk. You are a free being. You are a light being. Trust yourself to make the correct decisions each day and you will see how well you blossom into a true creator and provider. Then you will need no encouragement from others. You will live in the self-love that comes from knowing your own strength and that of the Supreme Being.

There is another path to enlightenment, which I will mention briefly. That is the path to the truth of all existence. It is a tricky path in that the truth changes as we speak. It changes with the tides and with the times. The truth is ever changing and so the person on this path is ever changing if he is to succeed. This is the path of the joker. He is always one step ahead of the game, and laughing at the mishaps of those who plan ahead. He can joke about life because he knows that there is no truth in seriousness; that all will change tomorrow and the seriousness will become a memory of an unknown event that will never be taken internally. So the joker is a saint in that he is never hurting, and a sinner in that he never understands the pain of others. He is forever laughing like a "crazy man" because he knows not the ways of others on different paths. His is a lesson to be learned, but it is not the path for everyone. Some people can glean some understanding from the joker's ways, and that is why he is so popular and in demand. He gives the world a new perspective that is rare and filled with humor. Know that the joker means well. He is like an alien on his own soil, and he can't understand why.

Now it is time to discuss why I have come here to talk to you. It is true that I wanted to clear my name from the prejudice that I see ensuing in those who follow my words. I am not here only on that mission, however. I have some other truths to instill and some to clarify. The first involves the issue of the hierarchy of the angels. There is no hierarchy in the eyes of God. There are no beings who are of a greater importance. There are none who rank higher in God's eyes. Some are given more responsibility based upon their desire to serve and their willingness to follow the order. Others are thrown into service by their actions. Still, God is One and Whole. God is all there is, and that includes everyone and everything. There is no one of greater or lessor value. So do not rank yourself or belittle yourself. Do not think that you are not worthy in the eyes of God. You are always worthy as one of his children. Do not think that you are better or more deserving than anyone else. You are neither better nor worse than any of God's children and shall not rank yourself as such.

Then there is the issue of responsibility. Those who are taken back to this life, to live on Earth, have a responsibility to their fellow humans. You are not alone on this plane—and for good reason. You are here to live life together. Remember this and look at how each of your brothers and sisters can serve the greater whole. Each person has a role here. By seeing this, you help your brothers and sisters find their own way. Remember that you are a child of God, so act accordingly. There is great responsibility in that. Take it to heart and do as you would to God himself. There is no other way. If you harm another being, you harm God. That is the end and beginning of it all. Remember it. Do not slap the face of God with your foolishness and idiosyncrasies toward hatred and mistrust.

Some people take the path that includes the love and understanding of all God's children. This is the only way to understand the heart of all hearts. To understand the love of all creation is to understand what it is to truly love. To understand how to love all of humanity is to know God's love. This is the greatest love of all and the only way to true redemption. For we redeem ourselves in our own hearts and the hearts of our fellow man. We look to others for guidance and seek to see the truth through the eyes of our brothers and sisters. When we are able to do this, we will see God in his entirety; for it is here that the truth lies—in the hearts of those who know and love God through his children. It is a true and honest path to liberation from the strife of the unknown and all-powerful evils of the mind.

There is an end in sight to the pure hatred that we have seen on the faces of some. This hatred is not an intention to do evil. It is a pure lack of understanding of love. The people who hurt from lack of loving are those who hurt others because they do not know love. I am not saying that you can take a criminal, show him love, and then he will become a saintly individual. No. There will still be the vacuum. He could still hurt you, so be wary of those who hurt others on purpose. They will never change in heart permanently. Do not punish them, but do not trust them. If they become too unruly and begin to harm others, ask God for assistance. Ask his servants, the Masters, angels, guides, and defenders. They will assist you. But as I was saying, the era of these empty-hearted individuals is coming to an end. I am not saying that there will be an end to criminal activity, but as the level of humanity rises, there will be an end to empty-hearted and deceitful individuals.

All men falter at times. But those who are empty-hearted and know no morals are rare—and becoming more so. You see stories on the news about mass murderers and killers. You see TV shows that make up stories about these types of people. The television and movie portrayals make it seem as if these people are common. They are not. They are a rare breed. Have faith in this, and as you look around, you will see that the level of humanity's love has risen.

People care about each other more than before. People are kinder in tougher situations. Be encouraged by this and take up the stand for more work in this direction. Be prepared to act as a warrior of the heart of God. Love your fellow man as God would and you will know what it is to love as God loves. This is truly the greatest of honors and blessings. When you do this, you will know no limits to what you can do and what you can say on this plane. You will be a true servant of the Lord your God.

You are not the only species on this planet that has become more enlightened. The consciousness of whales and dolphins has increased, also. Other species have grown as well, but it is not as noticeable. You give the dolphin a lot of credit, as if it were a mystical being. You look to dolphins and fairies for the mysticism you long for in yourself. Realize that you are a mystical being, as well. There is no being on Earth more mystical than mankind. You have the potential to soar to other planets, to soar to the very heart of God, just as all creatures do. You are much closer to God than you realize. Reach out, touch, and know your God. When you do, you will know the power that you possess to serve him.

Do not expect to see fairies and fiery brimstone in order to know God's love. It's much simpler than that. Look for God in the signs around you—here in the world you live in.

The spirit of the being known as Jesus

Freedom; Creating Your Reality

Thinking of the times when you were young, you seem to realize that you have lost a certain freedom. Is it the responsibility? Is it that you know more now or that you failed to see the truth? Now you are grown and remember only the freedom of not knowing. You are not free now because you now know that mankind is harsh unto itself, and the world is not an easy place in which to live. These were difficult lessons and you don't want to forget them. You regret your lost freedom, and value the fact that you no longer are hurt by others—or so you think. You hurt regularly, and over time it eats away at you. You hurt and you look away. You see only those who are as afraid as you are, and you resent that others in your world are not as enlightened as they "should" be. Such is the way of the unenlightened.

There are two things you must realize in order to enlighten yourself and regain the freedom of youth. The first is that you created your own pain; the others did not hurt you. You were not hurt because you misunderstood who they were. You were hurt because you took offense when the things they said were not honest, or the things they did were not as you would do them. You were hurt because you had a plan and the others in your life did not seem to go along with this plan. Children are not hurt in this way. Children are hurt by absorbing the negativity of those around them.

The second lesson to be learned is to not absorb the negativity. In order to prevent the negativity from permeating you, you must be the most positive person you can be. Do not look at the negative actions of others and take them to heart. Look at them and let them fall where they stand. Do not let the energy of others hurt you, and don't judge this energy lest you, too, be caught in its web.

You will regain the freedom of a child when you learn to live life one moment and one day at a time. Listen to those around you with an open mind. Do not listen to others through your heart. Give of yourself in proportion to what you feel is necessary and vital. Do not accept freely without scrutinizing it with your Higher Mind. When you let the information around you flow through the Higher Mind (not the analysis of judgmental thought) you will see that others are in the same place that you are, although they may speak from other places and other times. The people around you are no saints, and neither are you. We all make mistakes and try with all that we have. It is not for us to judge each other or pay our dues to those we feel have hurt us. We are only able to listen and move on. The hurt occurs when we take the words to heart. The words are meant for the mind.

The negativity can be filtered out here. Let the negativity stop before the third eye or sixth chakra. Let the idea permeate the ethers, but not your aura. You can filter what comes through to you if you pay attention. When you judge others, you are not filtering. Judgment requires the thought process that is often tied to the heart. It is nearly impossible to filter negativity at this level. You can't prevent it from hurting you.

Imagine a person who is yelling at you. Look at the person and watch how he moves, how he speaks, how he reacts to the energies around him. You will see patterns emerge, which are the same for all individuals when in this state. Observe impartially without listening to the words or taking them to heart. Then you will learn to recognize the stance and the posture of a person attempting to communicate through the veil of the negative. Learn to see this and you will be able to step back and protect yourself. Do not listen to the words or feel the energy. It is not for you. When people express such negativity, they are expelling the negative build-up that they feel. They are like an exploding pressure valve. It has nothing to do with you. It is a necessary form of ventilation for those who have no other form of release. Stay away from people when they are releasing in this way. Stay away from people who release like this often and regularly. There is no benefit in trying to soothe a pressure valve. The person venting needs to learn to control the steam and to mediate his internal environment to prevent this ventilation.

You are never free from the world around you, because you are a part of it. You are free to move in it as you wish. If you move in places that are comfortable and/or profitable to you,

you will be happy and feel the freedom of your youth. You had structure in your youth, as well. You had to go home at a certain time for supper. You had a bedtime and were expected to stay on the same street when you played. You couldn't hurt other people physically. These were all restraints similar to the ones you have now. You have time limits and deadlines. You have a body that needs care, and you know what you need to do to care for it. These are not restraints to freedom, but the necessary maintenance when you have a body. Do not feel hindered by them. Feel grateful that you have a body to care for. Many do not and they long for one.

You will feel freedom when you feel the freedom to be happy. You will feel freedom when you are moving into areas and places in life that are not negative and harmful to you. This will help you. If you are with someone who makes you work at being happy, you are with the wrong person. If it takes this much adjustment and acceptance of pain, you are not in the correct environment. Feel free to move on.

When you were a child you did not play with mean children. Do not do so now. You were alone if your only playmates were harsh to you. This was not easy, but you found no other way. This is still true for you. Play nicely with those you treasure and who are nice to you. Do not play with those who are venting too regularly or who cannot express their feelings in a kind manner. Do not play with those who hurt you by inactivity. If they let you down, stay away. Then you will find those upon whom you can depend.

It is very simple really. You will never be unhappy if you are in love with life and treasure the moments of it. When you allow yourself to do that which is unpleasant, or be with those who are rude, you are allowing yourself to feel hurt. You cause your pain. YOU hurt you. Do not close off to life and freedom. Reopen yourself to the amazement of awakening each day to new possibilities and the freedom to be happy in every way.

You create your reality. You have heard this before, but now realize it in its entirety. If you ask for something to happen, and it doesn't, you have either not allowed it to happen or you have asked for the impossible. The impossible can occur when you have asked for something that involves another being. You cannot ask for your life to center on another specific individual. Your life is your own to create. People must create their own lives. Do not ask that you be with someone in particular. Ask that you be with someone who has the characteristics you need to be with on that day. That can happen. Then you open the door for that person or another (who is in the same place as you are) to enter. If a new person comes to you, you will be able to relate to him/her much better than the person you originally asked for because he/she is in the same place you are.

Along the path we find that there are those who help us as we help them. This is the optimal arrangement. We must strive each day to be in service to ourselves and to God. That is the highest goal and affords the greatest freedom. With this aim there is no limit to what you can accomplish. Look to the path of light each day and give yourself the freedom to follow it. Like a child, you will find that the path opens to you as you awaken each day, and stays with you as you go to sleep at night. You are never alone and you are always in the grace of the

Almighty. Have fun with it and enjoy the path that has been created with you and your Lord's blessings. It is the ultimate happiness and joy.

The spirit of the being known as Jesus

Christmas and Easter;
Body and Soul Integration

Let's talk about Christmas. It's fortunate that my birthday is celebrated in the winter when the leaves are gone and the sky is easily seen. However, I do not accept that gift giving and light displays are connected with the belief in me. I don't see the relationship to my birth, as there were no lights of this sort at the time I was born. I was not in a well-lit atmosphere during any time of my life, and certainly not with green and red lights.

I'm not sure why people associate Santa Claus with my work and philosophies. True, I was giving; but I never gave toys. I didn't go down chimneys or rest during the summer months. I think this is a well-loved holiday and brings out the loving feelings in people. I'm gratified about that. I am not gratified that people feel the need to spend money on others to share the celebration of my birth. This is not a way to celebrate a holy day, if that is the intention.

Easter is more in keeping with holiness. The masses and the prayers, preceded by penance, are nice touches. There is more thought given to the religious teachings and less to buying things for others. Still, the Easter Bunny is again a bit out of the ordinary. Why am I associated with a bunny? Cute for the children—and the eggs could feed the hungry if they were not spoiled. But why summer hats and finery? Why not sobriety and joyousness at the resurrection? It is so strange that people are so rigid on the rules of the Bible, yet so improper on the traditions of the holidays.

I would like to suggest some new holidays. How about a summer festival, celebrating the sun and the light upon the earth? This could be a happy affair with lights of all kinds. The connection to the Holy Father (gender not intentional) could be made, and the light that the Supreme Being brings to the souls of us all.

The celebration of the fall harvest, as in some cultures, celebrates the bounty that is given by the Lord. In gratitude for God's bounteous beauty, let the leaves of color be the decoration for the holiday. We are so fortunate on Earth to know the beauty of the evolution of the planet. It is not common beauty. The sunset rivals the displays on any planet or world. The leaves of the trees that have given shade and oxygen to you are a gift and prayer for the growth of humanity. Why not celebrate this?

What are you celebrating when you celebrate my birth? Is it the reincarnation of the spirit of a being of light? Is it the fact that humans are able to birth enlightened beings? Is it that I am the savior and came to the planet on that day, or that I have been promised to you on that day? Perhaps it is the celebration of the birth of a new movement to understand the Lord. The latter is the most accurate. Enlightened beings are being born every day.

The savior is always among us in our hearts. We are our own saviors with the grace and enlightenment of the Lord in our hearts and souls. There is not one person who can save humanity. It must come from within all of us. The soul of the individual is but a part of the soul of the Lord. Is it possible for one part of the soul to be an enlightened being while the other parts flail and scream? It is not. We are all a part of one being. As I grow, you grow. As you grow, so do I. It is true of us all. We are each responsible for the growth and development of all humanity.

It may come as a surprise to some that their neighbor is their savior. The man on the street is their savior. The grocer, the baker, the shoe repairman or the robber is their savior. We are all a part of the same being. By feeding and understanding this we are able to help the whole body of humanity to develop.

Do not take responsibility for the growth of others. This is not my meaning. You cannot—I repeat—you CANNOT fix another person. We each must walk our own path. But in seeing God in others, we help them to see the God in themselves. We also must grow to be able to see the God in ourselves.

God's evolution is our evolution, and vice versa. It is possible for us all to understand this if we look upon how humanity has developed. We have grown from peasant beggars to developed nations. We have developed technologies to help the sick and have begun to help the poor in new ways. Yes, there are still beggars and criminals, but in less proportion. In past times there were more crimes of depravity and thoughtlessness, more selfishness and hatred. Hard to believe, I'm sure; but the world is not an easy place to grow up in. It is quite a challenge.

God's understanding is not always obvious when we look upon others, but the development of the race is a phenomenon worth noting. It is such a great undertaking to let the light of the Lord light the soul as self-understanding develops. This is not an easy task. All people are on a path of enlightenment and many do not know it. They are part of the Almighty and do not know it.

It's as if the Lord set up an image of itself in the form of little beings on a planet and then pretended that it was not a part of itself, just to see what would happen. Would new understandings develop? Would new ideas come of it? How would the cells (the souls) of the new part interact with each other without knowing the Source? How would they feed? Where would they turn and how would they proceed without the knowledge of where they came from? When these souls interact, the Lord sees itself and how parts of itself treat other parts. This is very informative. Is it any wonder that parts are eliminated? Do you expect that you would let a wart grow on your arm if it were stopping your circulation? The errant cells that do harm to the overall being are removed—plain and simple. There is no hell. There is only annihilation.

The hell that we refer to is knowing the pain and suffering within that causes sin. This is pure hell. But the good news is that there is an escape from hell. You alone can leave it by goodness and heartfelt love of others. The only way you can escape hell is to love others and realize that you are a part of the Almighty being. Responsibility to the God in you and others is the way of the warrior of the Lord. Are you a soldier or a wart?

The choice is yours.

There seems to be a discrepancy between what people feel about their bodies and what they imagine to be their minds. The body has an instinct that rules itself. It has genetic programming that is encoded to perform specific functions. This operates at the brain level, as well as at the lower body level. The brain controls all of the emotional and the physical activities, so some of the emotions you have are programmed at the body level and not at the soul level. There is confusion if the body is acting in a specific way that is unlike the needs or understandings at the soul level. Some examples of this are as follows:

There was a marathon runner in the late 1960s who broke his leg three weeks before the race. He went on to complete the marathon. Several years later, this man began experiencing strange sensations in his leg. There were cramps and tingles, and a feeling that his leg had a "mind" of its own. There was a sensation that the leg was not a part of his body, but belonged to someone else.

This individual had great control of his body at the soul level—so much control that he willed his body to complete the marathon at great expense to the leg. The body mind never recovered from this injury. The body was incredulous as to how this all took place. What the man experienced later in life was actually his own body's instincts recovering. The leg was finally healing after several long years. Until that time the leg belonged to his soul, in a sense.

Soon after these sensations began, the man had to have surgery on his leg. He'd sustained several injuries to the cartilage and bone tissue, which were never going to heal properly due to lack of correct attention—actual body attention. His leg had been isolated for so long that it was innervated to sustain activity without the help of the actual body. It took several years of reprogramming for this person to regain the use of his leg as he had once had it.

This was an example of the control that the soul has over the body. Here is an example where the body rules the soul:

A woman was hiking in the western part of Australia in the latter part of the 19th century. A large jackrabbit that was protecting its young attacked her. The soul knew that the rabbit could not harm the woman, though it looked vicious. The body would not hear of such a thing and immediately killed the rabbit.

It is important to recognize these different parts of the self. For some, the body mind is more prominent. For others it is the soul. The essential nature of the individual can be greatly affected by which mind they are in accordance with.

Sometimes you can be controlled by one and then instantly switch to another. Men in the sexual heat of adolescence often resort to the use of the body mind when relating to females. It's often referred to as hormones, but this is actually the body mind. The hormones do not think. The hormones affect the emotions and the responses to stimuli. They do not directly affect the brain's intellectual thinking. The intellectual thinking is programmed from birth. The body is given precedence due to the excessive stimulation of the emotional body through the hormonal activity of the body. This activates the body mind and poor judgment results, or judgment based on genetics and not Higher Mind.

What is the soul mind then, and how does it affect the higher learning of the individual? The soul mind is ruled by the experiences of the past lives of this soul, just as the body is ruled by the past lives of its genetic heritage. The soul has a direct link to all of its past lives. Not all of the lives are directly remembered, but all of the lives are remembered in the substance of the soul at the soul's "cellular" level. This learning on the experiential level helps the soul to act in each body, and in the times between lives. So some souls have different "truths" or experiential knowledge. You may sense this when you do not see eye-to-eye with another person. Sometimes you are both saying things that make absolute sense, but neither agrees with the other. Your soul experiences differ.

This is different from the times when body experiences do not coordinate. Inexperience on the genetic level results in prejudices between individuals, such as racial prejudice. The body is not accustomed to dealing with people who look different, talk different, etc. The body is a very protective creature by nature. It has evolved through several centuries of hardship. Times are often difficult physically for individuals, so the body learns to be suspicious and protective of itself. This is natural, but the results of this prejudice are often stressful to the soul. The soul of the individual may know that there is no essential difference between races—that a soul can inhabit several races and even different sexes. However, unless the soul being is experienced enough to bring its body's attention to itself, the soul will have little power. It is very painful when the body performs actions that are unjust. The soul watches in horror, like a being in a bubble, unable to control its vehicle as it reeks havoc on its environment.

The body has similar experiences when the soul controls it to the detriment of the body. People who exhibit this trait are often thought of as absent-minded. They may be clumsy or even get themselves into situations where the body would normally be wary. There are many hunters killed each year because they foolishly get in the way of an animal's wrath. The body would not allow itself to get into this situation. The body knows how to hunt and how not to be hunted.

So, what do we see here? The body mind and soul mind need to work together. How to do this? First be aware of the two minds. Listen to each. The body mind can be heard in sports. In stressful situations you might hear it saying, "Slow down. We might get hurt." You can consult the body in certain situations, such as in figuring the weather. Watch your instincts. The body knows what to wear and how to travel.

The soul mind is often easier to pinpoint. Some people first become aware of it as conscience. The soul mind is considerably more vast than this, but when you feel this twinge of conscience, talk to it. Watch it. Observe the minds and how they interact. Eventually you will be able to steer the two voices so they work as a team, both respecting the other. Then you can move in perfect harmony and eventually, perhaps, walk on water.

The spirit of the being known as Buddha

Time; Higher Consciousness; Color; Relating to Those on Different Planes

The concept of time can be disorienting. Have you ever noticed how when time "stands still" you are in a place of no tension or thought? It is true that when you are of a clear mind, your value of time slows. Time is almost stopped to the astral when you sleep. There is no concept of time on the astral plane, or dream state. You can move between periods of time in your dreams. Such is the case at the higher levels of consciousness. It's all just space. So we fly around merging with this and that, communicating here and there—an influx of energy into areas of need.

We don't need money where I am in the levels of higher consciousness, so there are no occupations. We don't need to eat food, so we are secure in our existence and do not have to put energy into this.

So how do I know what to talk to you about? I just talk and watch what happens when my energy merges with yours. Oh yes, we do have some merging going on. You merge to some extent with everyone you talk to or communicate with. There is a lot of interaction here. We're blended and are able to communicate through a word-like picture formation. You form words and they appear as pictures or scenarios to me. I then respond.

I would like to give you some information about how we on other planes communicate with you throughout your day. For example, before beginning this particular writing, Deborah and I had a discussion and learned a great deal together. We had traveled on the astral together and had many experiences where knowledge was shared.

This was all fun and delightful until the cat called and Deborah immediately stood up and went to her. The cat never speaks and Deborah sensed fear, or a call of need. She responded immediately. The cat was panicked over the energies floating around the room, sensing the somersaults and playfulness. It was as if she were seeing ghosts, her head turning this way and that as she watched the energies and spirits sliding around. Deborah comforted her, cleaned up the mess on the table, and returned.

That is exactly how life is in mindless silence. We are aware at all times; we are playful with others. We respond to calls immediately, do what's needed, and then move on. Sometimes we like to visit those we've been with in past lives; souls we've shared experiences with in the conscious arenas.

I can journey energetically into a class on yoga and transcendental thought. I can observe all of the students, their interactions and the information they are absorbing all at once. As a conscious spirit I have no desire to invade your space. Yes, there are some spirits on the astral who will invade your arena. You will feel them, though you may not know who or what they are. Suddenly you feel strange or feel unhappy or irritable. A weirdness that you do not understand permeates the air. You are not looking for beings, so you figure it must be something in you or in the person you're with. Look at the energy around you when you feel something of this nature. There may be an unsuccessful being in your arena who is stealing energy or inputting unnecessary energy into your space.

You can rid yourself of these beings by showering yourself with white light. Beings cannot see through this light and will not stick around. Yes, you can also shower the room. Remember to flush the light when you are rid of the force. That way you will be able to perceive more clearly. Light beings are not white, they are a golden iridescent color, which allows light to enter or leave. White light is as close to solid on this level as is any color. White light acts as a protective barrier.

Would you like a lesson on the benefits of different colors? Green is healing energy. Use it when you want to inspire growth and rejuvenation.

Red is an intensely inspirational light. It is very high energy and can drive a person to distraction if not used properly. This is important to remember when surrounded by red lights. These lights can cause the mind to trigger some animalistic chemicals, which will bring out the baser emotions. Some use this light during sex. This light will not enhance the connection between the two individuals. Instead it enhances only the animal passion and drive. Real enlightened sex—sex at its best—is not enhanced by red, but by warm orange/yellow, such as the light of candles.

Orange is warm and life giving. Orange adds a spirit of birth to the entity. Use it when you want to enliven something.

Yellow is the bright light of the soul. Yellow will heal on the soul level, and is the preferred color for beings who want to transmit messages to the souls on the earth plane. Yellow will also cure a hangover—really. Try it, if you can stand the light during a hangover.

Blue is calming and will help a person who is epileptic. It will also help those with sleep disorders. Blue will also calm the emotions and is a good color for helping those with schizophrenia or other neurological disorders.

Purple is a very inspirational light. If you want great insights to just pop into your head, turn on a purple light. This is why the "black light" became so popular when people were on drugs. It inspired great thoughts. Too bad these thoughts were not understood and were forgotten as soon as the drug wore off.

Do not use mind-altering drugs. They do not enlighten the soul, and they damage the internal organs of the body. Yes, there are rituals that can be performed that can open one's mind to insights not previously seen. These are to be done very seldom, however, with the understanding that the body is paying a price. The body is a rare and beautiful creature. Do not harm it with these unnaturally harsh substances. If you want to alter your mind, put your head under water. This will cleanse the thoughts. Alter your own mind safely with constant and diligent work on yourself. Breathing correctly will give you a lightness of being and presence to rival any drug, and you won't have flashbacks or bad "trips."

Every person on Earth has the potential for clairvoyance, clairaudience and clairsentience. It is just a matter of opening the mind enough to see, hear, and know the truth. We all have experienced times when we "knew" something that wasn't obvious or otherwise knowable. This sensation is not an intuition. This sensation is akin to opening a door just slightly and seeing a sliver of light. Traverse this path further and you will see that the door will open wide and you will be able to see the world around you to a new degree. How to do this is another day's topic.

The spirit of the being known as Malthasad

Energy Movement

I am Malthasad. I was an emperor of the Chinese Reich in the early 1400's before Christ. I was a guide and Master in that era. It is with great pleasure that I am speaking to you today. I know that many are interested in developing their awareness of the hereafter. Let me give you some information that will help you to process the energy from the other spheres, and to utilize it for your own growth.

The planetary influences of this era of time are aimed at opening the gates between the "spirit world" and the world of those who are human or in bodily form. We souls who exist in the astral or other planes are not restricted to one plane of existence. It is possible to move to other levels of reality. When this happens, we are able to gain perspective. No perspective is more valid than another; but with this flexibility, it is possible to gain understanding of a situation.

You, too, can accomplish this in your own way. Step into the shoes of another person for a split second by looking at his reality, and you will see that he is at another level of reality.

Then you can move around the room sampling the spaces of each individual. You will then gain a perspective of the entire movement of the situation, and not just the thoughts of one individual.

For example, you are in a crowd at a party. One person is talking about his relationship with his girlfriend. He is pessimistic and explains that they are having many arguments with one another. You step inside his reality for a moment. Do not read his thoughts, just look at the level of reality where he is. Then look similarly at each individual listening in to the conversation. Do not judge. Just observe how the dynamics of the group move the energy—who stays in the conversation, who leads, and who leaves. How does it flow and how do the participants interact from their level of reality?

By watching others in this way, you will begin to understand the dynamics of life's flow. You will see how the different levels of reality influence each other and how they are swayed. It is a physics example. You will see quantum leaps and spurts of chaotic energy. You will see the fire and heat from one level heating up the molecular dysfunction in another, which triggers the growth-like movement of the next individual. There are mechanics and dynamics that I cannot explain in full, but they will become apparent when you watch from this objective perspective.

The information from the conversation will become irrelevant to you as you watch the energy flow around the circle. You can then interject energy into the flow, as you feel necessary. You also can play with it and interject information from different levels to observe the result. You will then learn how to interact with others in a meaningful way, causing the conversation to spiral upwards. Your comments will remain unnoticed, but the level of the conversation will rise. The participants will rise to a new level of consciousness while this takes place. From then on, these participants will move at a slightly different molecular vibration, which will influence their growth.

Watch this and try it sometime. It may make "party talk" more fascinating. It is infinitely more fun than reading the playbills when standing in front of the theater. You will learn to shed sparks of light into people's conversations and atmospheres. Yes, you can do this subconsciously, or on the soul plane, as well. If you do not know the people, you can interject energy into the conversation and watch it move up a level. You are not being underhanded because they are the ones responding. They do not have to respond to you or your energy, but they most likely will. It is a choice they make consciously. Watch this. You will enjoy it.

The level of the people will be apparent as you watch them. By level, I mean the place from where they speak. Do they speak from the third level mind, which is the third chakra? Do you not know these levels?

There are seven chakras and seven levels of each chakra while a person resides in the body. These levels are not visible in the aura, but are sensed on the 3-D plane. They extend into other realms that are not visible. They have a certain vibration and a tone to them. You will recognize this when you watch.

Start with the third chakra. This is the area where people manifest their energy. Watch at the gym when people are working out. Some will be moving from a low, almost animal level.

Others will be moving with superb form—almost gliding. Listen for the "hum" or vibration, and watch for the luminescence of the aura. Then see this same differentiation in the other chakras. You will notice how one person responds to another.

This may become more complicated as you watch simultaneously which chakra and which level a person is speaking from. First start with just the levels. That will be clear enough. Just knowing that the levels exist will make them obvious to you—fun and games observing human interactions.

Next, notice that everyone moves at a different energy vibration. Each person has a tone or energy vibration which he or she alone moves to. There are also levels of energy usage. Some people are frenetic, while others are very lethargic. Watch how these levels of energy interact and see what happens when you add heat to a conversation. This is done by making a "warm" comment. Something with a loving heart will be warm. It can be humorous so that it is not as obvious. You can influence a conversation to move in a positive manner by interjecting heat in the correct intervals and relationships. Do not play with cold yet. Wait until you are adept. Cold vibrations can have unusual, surprising, and often unpleasant effects.

I have had much experience with this in my days on Earth. It was possible to watch others interacting in my council, as well as those in the streets of my villages. I could let them converse and insert positive ions into their space so that they could find their own answers in a meaningful way. They learned of their own volition, though not always consciously aware of the intervention. This is the best way for people to learn. Everyone on Earth grows in this way, always subject to Divine intervention and the addition of energy from the soul levels by your guides and angels. With these techniques you can learn how to heal from afar.

The spirit of the being known as Jesus

The Millennial Shift

It is now upon us, the millennial switch that we have been waiting for. It is extraordinary that it is happening when the suns of Jupiter are all aligned with the planets of the environmental galaxies. You are not sure about this. The galaxies are arranged around a central focal point—the Godhead—just as the planets are. They rotate slowly and vibrate swiftly as the energy breathes and recreates. It takes many forms too numerous to mention. The colors and sounds swirl and merge into extraordinary visions. You can see the millennial shift emanating into the stars as a radiant beam of light transforming all the surrounding galaxies with its golden glow. It is so enriching to watch this opening and awakening. It inspires all who are aware of it to move to a new level of reality within themselves.

The spirit of the being known as Anthropedes

Imagination

Many wonder about the role of the imagination and about how to differentiate between imagination and true interaction with other souls on the other planes. There are infinite sources of information available on other planes of reality and on Earth. You can pick up a book describing the last Armageddon, or travel to the east of Spain on a grand boat. The stories are readily accessible, with places for you to go and characters in your life. You can enjoy these games like video games. Run from the dragon, chase the giant snails, do whatever you like. As in a dream, you create your own reality.

These and other sources of information—which can also be referred to as information packets—allow you the opportunity to experience life on a grander scale. You can live vicariously without the trauma, but realize that this is not the true essential experience. You cannot learn from your fantasies or pleasures of the imagination in the same way that you learn from real life experiences. Fantasies and books give you a means to mirror your inner desires and needs, but they will never take the place of true living reality.

Now take the situation of talking to others on the soul or other planes. You can interact as you would in a fantasy, but you cannot control what the other person will say, or how or if he will respond. You are then living an actual experience. See the difference?

Do not judge either of these. Both of them have their uses. You may wish to experiment with other realities and see if something is pleasurable. Certainly you aren't getting the full picture when you are creating a fantasy or daydreaming. You are trying on someone else's photo opportunity. But you can see where it would lead in a make-believe world and then plan your dreams from there. Just remember your dream-come-true will include more and deeper experiences. In this situation, you can ask for your dream—but please realize that your dream-come-true will not be the same as you fantasized. There will be a whole other side of the picture—the other person's side and his/her dreams and fantasies. You can have a good handle on what could happen in certain situations, and could even predict certain outcomes; but you will never get the whole picture. The whole picture is created in reality in the moment and is more full than the imagination.

It is also possible to have discussions with the souls of people who are alive on Earth. You are truly talking to someone. You are talking soul-to-soul and will receive unplanned and unexpected information. This will give you insight into other people, what they desire, what their goals are, and where you fit in. You can also ask them questions about their work—even recipes, if you like. They won't tell you anything at the soul level that they don't want you to know. You aren't cheating or tying someone up. The soul is in control of itself (even more so than the other levels) and will not compromise itself. Be aware, however, that there is no body connected to it when it is talking to you. You are still getting only a partial picture. The person's ego and emotional/intellectual selves will certainly not go along with every scheme of the soul. If they did, there would be no more "game" to play. You can get an answer from the soul, but it may not pan out. There is an ego, after all, which will have a "mind" of its own.

Try experimenting with imaginative fantasies and also with talking to real souls. See what happens here and note the differences.

The spirit of the being known as Jesus

The Higher Mind; Honoring Your Own Truth

You are ready to experiment with transmutation of the energies and to foresee your own destiny to create your own reality or path. At this time the people on this planet are deeply in need of a real life assurance that they will succeed on their paths. They need reminders that they are recreating life as they live it. Many people are now finding their own truth, but attribute it to other beings or to God. They fail to see that they are the representatives of the living God. They fail to see that the actions they take and the words they speak are the reflection of the One.

Many people strive to be closer to God so that they can hear the Word to find out what to do and how to serve. You are soldiers of the Lord now. In order to serve, you must realize that whatever you say or however you act now, you are acting as a soldier of God. You are a part of God recreating itself—mirroring itself in its own image to gain information about itself. You need to take responsibility for your actions now so that you can create the living reality of the Godhead in present time.

We are the messengers of the Lord speaking to each other

and to ourselves. We hear each other through the many filters of the creation. Then we interpret it through our own experiences. The filtered message is often distorted and unreal in its present form. In order to realize the truth, one must learn to listen through the mind of the soul. The answer will come through more clearly here and will open one to the higher learning of the real creation.

For example, take a human being listening to a lecture or a sermon. The sermon may speak of topics familiar to the listener, but the words of the speaker are not heard directly. They are sent through the loop of interpretation, opinion, ideology, and finally through discretion.

Individual discretion is often different from real discretion. You interpret with the filter of the Higher Mind when you listen with the soul. It is here that you can pick up the inordinate wealth of information that is permeating every message on Earth. There are many messages to be given, like the intertwining cords of the notes of a song. A spiritual melody is being played out in every message given. The meanings intertwine and meld themselves to fit into the crevices of each individual mind. With the Higher Mind, you can hear all of the messages at once and decipher each meaning as it applies to each individual. Then you see how it relates to the higher purpose of the One.

It is like the writings of this work. Each Master speaks from the knowledge of his/her own insight, and each is speaking of the one path to the Lord. Each is speaking of the same evolution, but with different messages. These are all hints into the higher recesses of the soul, where you can see the truth for yourself.

The spirit of the being known as Jesus

Energy Transformation and Healing

For those who are interested, there is much to learn about energy transformation. It is a vast subject. The types of energy are endless and the uses just as endless. You have asked why the eternal energy filters through me to reach others. It is because I can float the particles throughout my aura and filter them in a vast array of energy fields, each specifically and vibrationally arranged to meet the needs of the individuals. This filtration and arrangement prevents burnout. The story of Icarus flying close to the sun and melting is similar to the effect the eternal can have on the unsuspecting soul. It is so finely powerful that you are not aware of its effect on you until you are one with it. Experiencing the Oneness in this way is not unpleasant. However, it can be a surprise if this was not your intention— and your intentions are an important part of the work of the eternal. So it is in the best interest of both parties (if two actually exist, which they don't) that you receive this energy in a filtered form.

There are other sources of the eternal that filter the energy.

The sun is a prime example, as is the moon. The stars are forms of light from the Lord, as is the heat of the volcanoes. Many beings can filter the energy to you, such as angels and archangels. The energy of the Lord works in many ways. It may seem destructive at times, but this is not so. It has not ruined something, but has recycled it into a new form. The energy of the Lord is always flowing and is an abundance of spectral energies all constantly creating itself in different forms.

For example, Deborah experimented with energy transformation the other night with a group of people. She watched a conversation occurring where the energy moved around the circle in a pattern and with a certain frequency. She then sent some warm, loving energy (non-personally) to one of the participants. The energy of the group suddenly changed. The people became quiet and more bonded. The frequency moved at a slower vibration. Soon they reverted back to their original pattern.

In this situation Deborah invented a type of energy that she thought would be pleasant and non-obtrusive, if not helpful. She did not want to negatively impact the others, or to affect their life lessons and form. The energy she chose worked in a positive manner and she was actually able to observe the experiment without it negatively affecting the parties involved. You see how she altered the energy. There is no end to the types of energy you can respectfully create. That is the beauty of it.

Healing is a form of transformation of energy to be used to permeate the organs and energy fields of the willing individuals involved. You can use a Healing Master (an out-of-body being who can heal) to create the energy for you, or you can drag your energy through yourself and into others. It is essential that you do not bombard others with your own transmittal. This is done when you transmit on your own frequency. Transmit on theirs. Find their vibration and transmit with a lighter, more positive illumination into the areas of pain or disease. The emanation will cause the areas that are inundated with other forms of energies to be purged, causing the inflow of the new energy to rise up and fight the disease. This is practical and very easy to do when you control your own energy.

When you do not control your own energy you can hurt yourself and others. You must remember to match the other person's vibration and to keep your own when the energy is in your body. This is essential. Do not generate the energy from within. This is too difficult and can be draining. You can channel the energy of the Lord through the moon, the sun, or through another form if you are unable to channel through God yourself. I can also help those who wish it, as can angels and the others mentioned. You will then be healed, as well, through the process.

In further discourse we will discuss how to channel energy to feed thoughts, dreams, and emotions to others. You will not be controlling or manipulating them. Feeding implies that you are giving what is required for their bodies specifically. If you want to heal someone, ask if they want it. This is always true when transmitting energy of any type to others. If you want to give out information verbally, ask the person if this information is wanted. If you want to help heal the body, ask first. If you want to share an experience, ask. Even if the person asks you first, clarify. He may be asking for something different from what he says or what you understood.

Take time each day to heal your body by sending God's energy through it. You can ask yourself first, too. Then see how you affect others. You will notice that the energy of the Lord adds radiance to your day and positively affects those around you.

The spirit of the being known as Jesus

Issues of the Heart

There are issues of the heart that need to be addressed. The heart is the cause of much pain on this plane, while being the door to infinite growth. Realize that pain in the heart is really the pain of growth. You are hurting because you are stretching. When people are in pain of the heart, it is not unusual to hear them say, "I am not capable of handling this. I can't do it alone." This is the key to understanding the healing process. It is not a matter of healing by yourself. Pain in the heart is healed best with the help of others. This is where the true bonding and realization of the unity of man and all creation begins.

Take a situation of a little girl of about five years old who loses her way in the park. She will cry in fear of abandonment. There is no way that the girl can heal herself in this situation. An adult comes along and helps the little child find her way. Now the girl is not only with her parent, she has learned the value of the assistance of others.

When a person is brokenhearted about the loss of a lover, it seems that there will be no end to the emptiness. If the person hangs on to the emptiness, the prophecy becomes true. If a space is opened for another to enter, it is realized that there is love in all, and it is realized that the truth is in the unity. True love exists in the unity of the One.

It is essential to realize that to assist another you must not invade his or her space or aura. You are there to assist with guidance if asked. The guidance you give must be specifically related to what the person is going through. If you relate it to your own experience you are not relating to his or her space, you are relating to your own. You are not giving information about the individual; you are giving information about yourself.

If you want to assist, you can tell the person what you see about the experience. Describe the experience like you are looking at a painting or reading a book. Show what you see. Then the person can take the information and use it to his or her own benefit. If you are incorrect, he will correct you. If he is angry about what you saw, you were probably correct. If he is hurt, it is not your problem. It is not your responsibility if the person asking for information is hurt by it. You gave what was asked.

Try to tell what you see positively without direct confrontation. You can talk around the subject and then narrow down to the basic point. For example, take the man who is continually trying to please you—but what he is doing is not pleasant. You can point out that you recognize how he is trying to please you and how thoughtful it is. Next you can point to specific actions that were beneficial. Then without putting a judgment on it, you can draw attention to a specific incident that was not productive. You might say something like, "You brought the groceries in and that was kind and thoughtful. You laid them on the counter and did not tell me about it, so the ice cream melted." The truth may not be pleasant, but in this context it is palatable.

An appropriate teacher does give advice based upon what she (or he) sees. She does not suggest things to you unless you ask—and she does not hypothesize. A true teacher gives information based upon what she sees. This is different from someone giving you hypothetical information based upon some imagined or past experience.

I saw a teacher tell a child that she was wrong in telling her parents to go to hell. The teacher told the child that the parents might just go there because of what she said. In reality, her statement has no effect on her parents' journey. The child was being hostile and the teacher could have pointed out that the hostility was inappropriate in that it caused pain in her parents. That would be an accurate observational analysis that would be useful in future situations. As it was, the child took the advice about "hell" to heart, and although she may or may not use the word or phrase again, the opportunity for learning something of far-reaching importance has passed.

The spirit of the Healer Morraux (More-oh)

Human Illness & Healing

There is much to be learned about the care of the body. Even after thousands of years, the human mind has yet to figure out its idiosyncrasics. There is so much the body can do that has yet to be discovered and explored. For example, the stories of people transporting themselves to other parts of the planet are true. You can also hear much farther than you expect. It is a matter of expanding your perspective of what can be accomplished.

Let us take the example of human illness. People now believe that germs permeate the body and cause illness. This is not entirely true. Germs or other aspects of the Life Source are constantly invading your territory. You fend off the invasions of bacteria, as they are insidious and tend to want to take over any area they claim. You have found that viruses (which are not actually beings, but are a means for the genetic codes to reform) "invade" and alter the body in a negative manner. What you don't realize is that their main function is to alter the body in a positive manner. The virus is a code of DNA that can be used by the body to alter its genetic structure. The body does this on its own. The genetic structure is well encoded over time and needs little adjustment, but on a daily basis the body uses parts of viral DNA to perform certain functions.

Illness is actually resistance to foreign bodies, not an over-taking of those same bodies. The human experience is one of continual growth and development. The body is also growing and developing, although it is also using up parts of itself at the same time. Some parts are no longer needed.

The female reproductive organs are the most obvious example of this. They stop working when no longer needed. The organs do deteriorate to a certain extent when no longer used. If you stop eating sweets, your pancreas will begin to slow down. If you then want to eat a lot of sweets, or even increase your intake, you will need to add sweets slowly if you want to stay well. In this way the pancreas will gradually grow to adjust to the change in diet.

Your body can handle any type of food if given time to adjust to it. Not eating meat is a common fad of late. The body does run more swiftly and cleanly for certain activities if not eating flesh. However, if you lived in the arctic regions of the planet, your body might do better to eat meat and/or fish to sustain the metabolic and heat-producing requirements of the body. Although, if you had been eating only vegetarian foods, you would need to slowly adjust to eating flesh.

With this in mind, let us discuss illness. Illness, as stated, is a resistance in force in the body. The resistance is usually created in the mind. A flu virus affects someone and gets publicized. Everyone on the planet is made aware and put on guard for this virus. When the body intercepts it, it fights it and a war erupts.

Remember to listen to the signs of your body. Many try to manipulate the body by pushing it beyond its capabilities, or trying to accomplish tasks when it is tired or overworked. It is so simple, yet so overlooked. Your body is a well-functioning machine with a computer brain that runs it to perfection. If you feed it poisons or foods it doesn't want, if you exercise beyond its capabilities, if you forget to feed it or put it to bed, you will become ill. Any machine would do the same. So in this case the illness is not from resistance, but from ignorance. And that is the end of the situation. The body rejects the actions that created it and shuts down. The mind may have its fill or the sexual emotions will have a party at the expense of the rest of the body, but it will catch up with you and you will go down. It is so simple. Do what the body needs you to do for it and it will function to perfection for many years, perhaps even centuries. Treat it poorly and you die.

Listen to your body. Feed it what it wants and only that. Feed it only the amount it wants and not more or less. Give it rest when it requires it and exercise it to expand it to its fullest potential. Love your body as you would a lover and it will take very good care of you. You can then begin to explore the other talents I've mentioned.

The key to learning the idiosyncrasies of the body is to listen to its basic needs. When you do this you will begin to sense its inner secrets. It will show you parts of itself that you have not sensed or seen. You will become more intimate with its talents and shortcomings, and will then be able to use it to its greatest capacity. Athletes are very attuned to this. You see how well they push themselves to extremes, but also provide proper rest and stretching. It is all a very attuned game, if you want to think of it as such.

You may wonder about how to rid yourself of a disease (dis-ease) after it has "caught" you. When you are exhausted, you may be more resistant to certain events taking place in your life. This resistance is interpreted in your body as dis-ease and it starts to break down. If you do not rest the body when it needs rest, it is not able to recover without the assistance of drugs and the help of Healing Masters—as well as a very strong will not to be ill for long.

You can push the illness out of your body by force of will. That is not easy to do.

You can push your body beyond its limitations so that you can experience what you desire. Then you must repay the body with much healing energy. Do healing meditations, eat impeccably, feed it well and heartily, and give it plenty of time to rest and recover. Thank it and appreciate its effort. Then put yourself on the path of wellness.

In order to remain healthy, one must learn to resist nothing and pay attention to the health and needs of the body. To not resist is to accept what life offers. If you are presented with a situation you do not want, realize that you created the situation. It is yours. If you resist it, you are resisting your own efforts and causing an imbalance. To change the situation you must find how and why you brought the energy or situation into your life. Then either change what you've asked for, or ask for removal of the situation.

For example, let's say that you have asked for a raise in your job. You get it, but you have so much more responsibility and time at work. This becomes very stressful and you do not know what to do. You become weak and tired; you become angry and ill. How can you change this situation? You must first realize that although you asked for more money, you did not anticipate the increased work or responsibility because you overlooked this. You can now ask for the situation to change by either making less money again, or having the job change in some way to give you more time and less responsibility. Visualize a new employee being hired, or less work being slotted to you. Do not be angry or sad. This is resistance. Change it by bringing in new energy and asking the grace of God for a new situation. This will happen for you if you believe it will.

Another example would be if your husband is angry and acts out a lot. You are resistant by being hurt and angry with him. Look inside yourself. What have you done to cause this, or open the door to it? Do you expect this behavior? Do you feel less self-worth and so bring in this energy? Feel worthy of good behavior and know that it will come. It will. Your husband will most likely change. If he does not, you will change the situation based on your new energy and higher level of understanding of self-worth.

If you have an illness, you have either overworked or underfed your body, or you have fought against your own life situation. Look to yourself and cure yourself.

The spirit of the being known as Samson

Relationships

It is said that in order to love someone, we must learn to accept and be a part of him/her. This is not entirely true. A true love is one who is admirable, respectable, thoughtful and considerate of our needs. The person does not have to have the same interests at heart or even the same beliefs. It is only important that the individuals are aware of the impact each has on the other, and to minimize the resistance each feels to the movement of the other on his or her individual path. There is much to be said for two individuals from different views who link together, if they can share ideas and learn from each other. This is only possible with trust and complete respect.

Imagine how it would feel if the person you are with is not of the same mind and tried to convert you. Then picture the same person with respect and admiration for you. The ideas and opinions would intermingle seamlessly and flow together into one whole. This is the purpose of all creation and the Higher Purpose of love on the earth plane.

I am not suggesting that one should seek a person who is

completely of different orientation and mindset. However, people who look for those who are like themselves—who can become a part of themselves—will soon become bored and restless. It is like seeing yourself in the mirror. Would you stare at yourself all day? I hope not. You want to interact. You want a filter of different orientation to view things in a new way.

Some traits to look for in a mate or companion are fortitude and strength, commonality of purpose, common likes in hobbies and entertainment, resistance to changing values, truth and honesty, and variance of opinion when presented with new suggestions. It is important that the individuals are on the same path—one of lightness and purpose, or headed in the same direction in soul. This will ensure a proper alignment of the information. Otherwise there will be dissonance.

Respect your mate. Respect. That is so different from accepting them. It is the ability to look to them with light and love and honor, no matter the goal or task. Attitudes change, but values must remain intact. A person with solid values and a sense of purpose is worthy of any mate, no matter the opinions or state of mind.

Remember that there are those who are seeking other purposes in life. There are some who want stability. Others want wealth or children to raise. All of these are valuable to the individual. However, one who is on the path to true awakening can be with someone who has different goals. He can remain true to his own goals or abandon them with the true intent of finding an individual with whom he can align on the path. This alignment will be supportive when presented in a kind and nurturing environment. Both individuals can benefit from the information given by the other and can learn to process in a new way, as well.

Let us use an example. Imagine two individuals who meet on a ski slope. One is from a recreational orientation. The other is from a spiritual and intellectual path. It would appear that the two are not compatible; but they are both sound of heart and purpose. They are both wise in their respective worlds. They have paid close attention to the goings on in their own worlds, and have learned a great deal. It would seem that they have nothing in common—but they have the world in common. They enjoy the same activities and also enjoy the energy of the other. Being together gives each the opportunity to experience another whole world without living it. If they stay open to each other's perspective, and listen with intent to the lessons the other has to teach, each of them will benefit a great deal.

Intention is also not as important as one would imagine. For if both are unsure about the nature of the relationship and allow it to form in time as it may, all the better. One must be open to new possibilities. These two will live each day as it comes and create their own environment and sentiments. They will listen to each other and pay attention to how they each process information. Then the two will be twice the people they once were.

Someone might say, "I want to share ideas and common insights with someone." Insights are not limited to content. Another person can have the same understanding, but in another area. The perspective they then give on the topic is of a much broader range than that of someone who is of the same orientation in life. If they are both open-minded to the perspective and information of the other, they will gain a great deal.

Another might say, "I want to be with someone I have

things in common with." These two people have much in common. They like athletic activities; they enjoy the outdoors; they are alike in body and spirit. This will be enough to keep them moving in the same direction and enjoying each other.

Take two other individuals. They each are intellectual and enjoy the same activities. They have common backgrounds and experiences. They process information in a similar manner and have the same viewpoints. It is easy for these two to get together, but difficult to stay together without bringing other people and experiences into the relationship. They will soon tire of hearing the same opinions. They will run out of topics to discuss. The discussions of daily events will revolve around the same things. One person will relate the events of the day, knowing full well what the other has to say about it. The opinion and advice of the other are known before even asking. Soon the conversation is stale. The two will then resort to adding company to improve the energy of the conversation. Irritability may be common. Soon they will be two people going separate directions, whether they stay in the relationship or not.

Life will always be exciting and informative for two people who have different experiences and orientations, but who are on the same path and spiritual journey—whether knowingly or not. Life will offer new possibilities and combinations of events that otherwise would be impossible. Remember that it is essential that the two be open and interested in the other's viewpoint and processing. It is important to take note of how the other person approaches a situation and moves in it. Also, it is essential that one does not become impatient if the other does not act as he/she does. That person cannot because each is learning from the other.

One person may be from an elite background, adept at manners. The other may be from a warm and compatible environment where family love comes easily. One will teach social graces and skills, the other family values and love. This is a wonderful trade-off.

One may be from an athletic background, pushing the body with knowledge and connectedness. The other may know how to hone the intellect and mind to reach new understandings. This is an opportunity for both to see that tolerance is not appropriate, but rather true respect and enjoyment of the other, anticipating a new and wonderful outlook on the world. Each will take the information of the other and incorporate it into his or her psyche, becoming new and fuller individuals in their own right.

Soul mates are different aspects of the same being. It is not as important what sex or what nationality unless this is an integral part of the lessons to be learned. So a soul being can take on two aspects of itself at once, in different parts of the planet. It is rare that these parts would meet, as they are already part of the same person. However, there are times when one would want to be with oneself in a different form in order to see life from two perspectives at once. This is true of souls who are looking to move to a new realm soon and want to process much information at once. It is also true of souls who need security and to know that they are cared for. The soul learns to care for itself in its entirety, and therefore becomes whole and complete in its self-love.

This meeting of the souls, or soul, is monumental to the being. It may or may not be obvious at first, but soon the individuals will see the commonality of each, and through this, learn to accept the differences. Thereby the two parts of the soul learn to accept each other and love all of humanity through each other. They become one in spirit and in holy love. This is a blessed event and marks the beginning of the soul in whole as it moves to the spirit realm as a guide and Master. It is celebrated with great rejoicing on the other planes.

There are times when the souls do not recognize the oneness of themselves. It is not important. The love of one for the other, the learning and self discovery—these are important. It is essential to respect all you see. Remember it may be another part of you in disguise. If not, it is still another part of the soul of the Almighty and essential in the scheme of the ever-unfolding nature of life. Enjoy it and cherish the time you have with each other, whether you are the same or different. You are all essential and worthy of respect and admiration.

Do not give away any part of your soul to others. You will be crippled and will no longer serve appropriately. No matter the love and delight you feel, another is another. We each have an essence of spirit that is our own. Share yourself by giving love and being a light to those around you. Let no one take what is not theirs. They cannot use it, and it will poison them and those around them.

The spirit of the being known as Buddha

Handling Adversity

I was once a beggar, you know. Imagine my predicament. I totally depended upon the kindness of others for years. It was very enlightening. I saw how special and wonderful everyone really is. Oh yes, there were those who mocked and scorned me, but there were so many who fed me and livened my day. I thought myself worthy because I saw that the act of giving is the greatest gift of all. When we give it to others out of the love in our hearts, we shine. Love is the core of our being, and letting it shine is our greatest legacy.

For example, today Deborah helped several people to feel the power of kindness and love. She didn't make the luggage attendants feel guilty because they lost her luggage. She helped them to see that they can do more if they keep trying to find it. She shed light on a problem situation without making those people involved feel that they were bad or evil.

She was not at all hostile to anyone, even though the pharmacist was late, the bank put her on hold for twenty minutes, and the baggage claim people still hadn't called her back. She's not angry with them, but is allowing everyone to BE. When you allow others to BE, you'll find that they often can be their most helpful and kind.

Some would be devastated by the mishaps that Deborah experienced today, yet she just continued on. This was motivating for others. She focused on what she had to do while not getting upset by what she had to do, and was a perfect example of "being here now" and responding to each moment.

Today Deborah showed herself and those around her that life goes on and you will just pick up the pieces as they show up. She was like a warrior who's been injured in battle, fighting the pains and bruises while taking care of the tasks that need to be accomplished. Bravery occurs each day and not only by those in uniform.

Each day people live their lives and cope with issues and problems as they arise. Each person handles them differently. Many handle them well, and in the process, become stronger and wiser. We are all warriors in God's eyes. We take our battles and we turn them into victories, though our hearts are plundered and sore. We take our lessons and use them for further good; and we will learn to appreciate that we are not fighting to stay happy. We are living to be that way. We are the warriors of the souls that possess us, and it is our love that fuels each and every endeavor.

The spirit of the being known as Michael

Universal Messages

My topic today is on the wisdom gained from others. You are always wiser when you are in control of your own learning. It is important to honor your own truth and to allow your own Higher Self to control your learning, but what happens when you also open yourself to allow the learning to come from God in any form?

There are messages surrounding you all of the time. It is easy to ignore them. People ask questions, but refuse to believe the answers. Often an answer is too simplistic and therefore seems too trivial. For example, a woman asks to communicate with her mother who's been dead for over twenty years. She asks a question, "Dear mother, if you are listening, please tell me why you were late to my party. If you had just come on time you would not have been killed in that car accident, and I would be with you today." The woman puts this out and the question reaches the aspect of the Universe known as this woman's mother, who attempts to get her answer through.

The next day the newspaper is placed on the front steps of

the daughter's home. It would be helpful if the article stated that a woman was prevented from involvement in an accident because she was listening to a broadcast concerning current traffic patterns. Actually the headline reads, Traffic Patterns in the City Delay Important Meetings. This message is obscure and not picked up by the daughter, so the mother tries another method. She arranges for a phone solicitor to call and ask how traffic patterns in the city affect her life. However, this message isn't heard, either.

So next there is another opportunity. The daughter is driving home and there is a tremendous traffic problem directly near the accident area where her mother had been twenty years earlier. Again the message is clearly telling the daughter that the mother was late because of traffic problems. The mother can't speak directly to the daughter, but she's giving messages to answer the question.

In the headlines the daughter sees that traffic is a problem. She sees that traffic broadcasts are forthcoming. She sees that accidents in the area near her house are preventing drivers from reaching their destinations. Now if the daughter had put these three incidents together instead of fretting over the fact that she received a telemarketing call, was delayed in traffic, etc., she would realize that the message was there. This is how life speaks to you.

There are many incidents each day where prospective angels, spirit guides, and others speak to you. It is not necessarily appreciated or heeded because there is no one message that answers the question directly. However, when you put them all together, you'll see that there is a pattern here.

Look for patterns. Look for information coming in groups of three. Span your memory for information that is tied to aspects in your life now. If you write it down, you will find it helpful. It is not important how the message comes to you. The out-of-body spirits are not as adept as you are in communication. They are not prepared to speak to you, nor could most people handle angels popping into visibility all of the time and giving answers to the questions of the Universe.

It is a ripe time for personality change and new horizons. Areas to be wary of are feelings of seniority, or problems gleaned from low self-esteem. It is not your position to wonder why people act the way they do. It is only important that we recognize each person on the journey, and honor his or her method of partaking in life's abundance.

The spirit of the being known as Jesus

Self-love

You will look at me differently when you are in love with yourself. You may look to me for guidance; look up to me for truth. Now you look at me as one who knows. When you know self-love you look at yourself as one who also knows. I may be more experienced and perhaps more eloquent. You, however, have as much to offer the world. Each person has as much to offer, and with self-love as the backbone, everyone will successfully contribute to the growth of humanity by simply BEING.

There is no difference between living life on Earth and being with God. When you let go to the Will of the Eternal, you truly know God's light and learn to co-create with the God-force. It is then that you become the manager of the energy that runs through your life.

Take today, for instance. Deborah was awakened at 5:00 a.m. and so began to write. She was not pleased to be awakened from sleep. She was not even totally awake, but she answered the call to arise, and she had an insight that taught her the importance of loving herself.

A tree grows slowly when it is subjected to harsh winds, brash sunlight, and cold. When people are subjected to continual beatings of anger and negativity, they are like the tree in poor living conditions. God provides miracles to sustain us under these conditions. However, without self-love this manna falls on deaf ears and hearts. There is no love gained by the person from the experience.

It is timely to note that there are many who are learning this lesson now. You will notice that most people feel like they've failed because the economy is failing. There is a downturn in the economy at this time, and it directly affects the people in it. If you direct your love onto material objects and judge your worth by those possessions, you risk failure. When you realize that you are not your stuff, you will see that you are the master of yourself in your own life. A street person or a millionaire, you are still the same person. Your successes do not define you. You are as you are now. When death knocks on your door it will not say, "What have you earned in this life?" It will say, "Who are you?" It is best to say with pride and love, "I am that I am." Then you can look death in the eye and move with it to a brighter world.

Now is not the time to be evaluating your place in the world. The world is shifting. The economy is shifting. The people are rearranging themselves. How can you judge yourself when compared to a shifting mass? You can only look at yourself in spirit and know that you are fine and perfect as you are. When this is done in times of great stress and under the pressure of great obstacles, you will find that you are healing yourself and gaining a tremendous amount of strength.

What is strength but self-love? There is no more to that sentence. You look for more, but it is a fact. Self-love is love of God. You are a part of God. If you do not love yourself, you cannot love God and all of its parts.

As you greet other people, your intention should be to meet with them—not merge with them. It is an important time on Earth now. There is a need to meet and heal and support each other. The connection will feed you whether you are with an acquaintance, a mate, or a friend.

If you meet another and offer a heart filled with self-love, you are offering a gold mine of information and energy. If you present a heart that is empty of self-love, you present a vessel that needs healing. Life is not meant for the filling of vessels through each other. Life is meant for giving of oneself through the taking of God's love and spreading it to others. Do this and you will never fail.

The greatest healers and teachers were poor. I was not monetarily successful, as you know. I was a carpenter, yet my name has lived on for thousands of years.

Buddha was not a saint in costly robes. He wandered the streets like a beggar. Do you think he valued himself on his accomplishments? No, he was truly a person in his own right who looked at others with love of self and God. The power of his love spread. It is the only real power we all have. Use it. Wield the sword strongly and with all your might.

Some will ask, "How do I love myself?" It is not so difficult. Just feel love. Remember a time when you were happy. Look at the sun during a sunset and love the beauty. Find some excuse to love, even if it's external. When you do, you will find a person who is capable of loving. Turn that love toward your heart and you will learn the true meaning of healing your heart. Love is the key and the answer to all questions; and it starts with you.

The spirit of the being known as Michael

The Power of Prayer; Living in the Moment

It is a strange time in the history of humanity. It is a time of great transition. You are not as sure of the outcome. It is hard to see the future when you are locked in the turmoil of the present, whether the turmoil is yours individually or on the planet. Take time each day to pray for yourself and the planet, and you will heal yourself and others.

There is great power in prayer, and it is important to have an intention. Your intention can merely be to promote the highest good of all humanity and heal the wounds of the oppressed. You can do global healings each day as part of your meditation.

You are waiting for an answer, but don't know the question. Life is a question. It is always asking, "What next?" You sit and meditate, or walk on the beach. You are mesmerized by the beauty, or in awe of the power of the creative force, but there still nags at the back of your head, "What next? What am I doing here?" It is not enough for you to just BE. You feel the need to be something, as if you are nothing unless you are being something or doing something. It is not hard to see that you will always be on edge this way because you are never complete. There is always a pressure to be more and do more. There is a need to perform and the performance is always lacking because it is never complete.

Many feel an obligation to perform, and feel a restlessness to eliminate the negativity and resistance in their soul. You may believe that you must grow or you will wither. This is a true fact, especially on Earth. However, what if growth is not as you see it? What if growth comes in releasing the need to perform, releasing the need to grow? Perhaps there is another level of activity that is not obvious in the physical, and you only need to relax into it to become enlightened.

How do you achieve this state? The answer to all questions is to relax and be in the moment. Eat of life, and fulfill yourself and others as you feel the need. There are many avenues that lead to growth and enlightenment. When you are on your true path, you relax in the moment and do what you truly feel is best for you. There is no time for unnecessary obligation. There is no need for rest when you are not tired—no need for food when you are not hungry. Your life will take on a new rhythm and you will be in tune with the harmony of life in God's joyful abundance. You are not a spirit in a body. You are a spirit AND body. You travel in and out of body. Be in your body and do what you want to do while there. It will be obvious. If you are uncomfortable, do something else. If you feel a nagging to do something, do it. If you are restless and uncomfortable, move on.

Be not afraid to be one with God. You can show the world what this is like. It is great to be with someone who is in tune and dedicated to the path. Others will recognize this. Be there for them.

The spirit of the being known as Mary

Love

It is time to speak of love. Love again and again and again. I cannot speak too much about love, as everything is channeled through love. You are not as aware of how this works as you think. It is not just energy that runs through your veins. It is "loving" energy. You are unhappy and upset when you don't have this energy. That is what you are seeking. You do not seek to have love in your heart; you seek to have love surrounding you. You are aware that there is love in the world. You see it all of the time and everywhere. It is not uncommon to find it in others or in your dreams. To find it in your heart, however, is another challenge.

You look to love as a way to heal yourself. It is not a healing salve; it is a life energy that needs to be channeled through your veins, your heart, and your mind. Keep love moving through you and there are no questions of pain or sorrow. There is compassion for those who do not know love because they are the ones who truly suffer.

Love is not something you earn or learn. It is not a transient passing fad, like romance or lust. It does not vary when you're angry or sad. It remains constant like the sun on a rainy day. The sun is always present. You can tune into it or not. When storms come, it becomes more of a challenge to tune into the sun. When strife and hardships occur, it is difficult to see the love that surrounds you. Still it is there.

There have been many difficult times in life. There have been many eras of great suffering. Even now people suffer in anguish. Those who are without love are in pain the most. It is not the starving who suffer most, but those who are starving from love. How many times and how many stories do you need to remind you that love is the answer, and not fame, fortune, status, or adventure? How many people say it, but do not understand it? Love is around you and in you. Find it and it will answer all of your questions.

You will know when you find love. It is like being alive on the Earth. You know you are alive and in a body. When you feel the love in you and around you, you know it. It is a part of you.

Take the time to sit for a moment, close your eyes, and breathe. Think back to a time when you were young. Perhaps you were playing in the woods or in your yard. See yourself there now. Feel the sun on your body. The sprinkler or swimming pool water surrounds you. The birds are chirping in the distance and the cool grass is under your feet. It is soft and nurturing, and you are very aware of the soil beneath the grass.

You know the Earth is your home and your support. Feel it under and around you. The sky is blue and clouds are floating by. See the puffy ones? You are alone and you are whole. What do you feel? Are you concerned about others and whether you are loved? Are you thinking of the future and how you should be? No, you are whole. That is love. True, it doesn't have the flare that incites the senses into hormonal bliss. From here, however, you can build a love and sensuality that moves beyond the petty nuances of loving in the purely sexual form. From here you can experience another while knowing the bliss and serenity of being on the planet, supported in love by the Mother/Father.

You are asking for the love of others to support and defend you. That is not necessary when you are supported and loved by the Mother/Father. That external validation is not needed when you know the wholeness of the love that surrounds you and is in you.

The outer forms of self-love do not fulfill you. You are not fulfilled when you sit in the feeling and feel the pain of no return. You feel the pain of not knowing who you are and not knowing where you want to go. It is the pain of growing beyond your true spirit. You feel that you are not supported and in love because you are not in your body and loving the Mother/Father in you. You are not fulfilled because you are looking for others to fulfill your needs.

You can create a reality now and in the future. If you long for contact and support, you are wasting your energy. You already have this. You already have someone to talk with, someone to love you, someone to care for you and to listen to you. You have all eternity around you to support you. You have all time and space to send you into creation. You are not alone and you are not in need. The need you feel is from not knowing the love of the Mother/Father in you.

This is where the creation begins. You can create from this place and then your creations will be based in love. When you create from this place, you are nearing your heart's desire. You are now creating a life as filled with love as it is based in love.

Experiment with this. Sometimes you might imagine what you would like to do. Plan for it, and then go from there. Other times you might experiment in the moment and play with what you have nearby. It is not difficult to change boredom into bliss. Merely smile and do something you enjoy.

You may have obligations, but it does not serve you to be stuck and unhappy. If you are unhappy with your life, plan your way out of it. Chart a course toward happiness. If you are restless and unhappy, envision a future of happiness, and then take the necessary steps to get there. Look for the signs from the Mother/Father to support you. You can have whatever you want. You see the goal and then go there. That is all that is required.

In times of strife, look at the lessons to be learned and move to the light, feeling the love of all within during these stormy times. Honor your desires and move in the physical world to put your dreams into reality.

That is the way to happiness in eternity. It is not unusual to be unhappy, or even depressed. It is a natural sign that you need to move in a new direction. Take your energy and build on it. Release the depression and fly out of it. Push aside the cocoon of your sadness and look to the light in the sky. You will see a new dream and a new reality. You imagine it. You can even taste it. You know it's there. This is not just a dream. It is the budding of a new reality—the start of a new life. Do not discount it. Take it and nurture it. Believe in it and cherish it. Take your time with it and flourish in the knowing that it can and will happen if you allow it and work for it. Work, in this sense, means allowing yourself to unfold into the new reality and dream.

Release the binds that are no longer usable in the new life. Look at behaviors and ways of responding to life. Look at how you know that you are full and satisfied. Recognize that you need new sustenance, and find it; crave it. Look for it in all you do. Find the true path and travel it, one step at a time. Plan and amend the plans. Act and then plan some more. You will find your way to the new reality with the love and happiness of the Creator in you. You will know that you are on your path when you find that you are farther along each day than when you started. You will see that you are not alone, and you will continue to strive to assist others to see your light and movement so that they, too, might move from their drudgery.

Life will take on new meaning as you move from your dreary sustenance to the fuel of the soul—LOVE. You will feed and find love within and around you. It will support you and will offend no one. It will bind you and will sustain you, and you will know no other love than the love of the Creator. For this is the only love that exists. The lust and the remnants of past idiosyncrasies will fall away when you know the true heart of the Creator. Then you will learn to see this love shining out from the eyes of all you meet. For it is there, even if you do not know it. Love sustains us all.

Some are not approachable and are hidden in fear. Look into the eyes of love in everyone and you will find it. Even in strife and anger, look for the love that resides in the moment and you will find a way to reach your true heart. For that is your aim. You are striving for your humanity to match with your loving nature. Listen to the words of the prophets who said, "All who reside here are sons and daughters of the one true God. And the One resides in the hearts and souls of all who are present."

Do not expect to find love in your heart, but feel it in your soul and in the souls of all who are present. The heart and soul are one and the same, and it is here that you will see the truth behind the meaning of the word God, for God is love. Love is all there is. If you learn to see this, you will know that there is no wrong to be done, nowhere to go but into the arms of God in love.

Truly you know this to be so. You are aware that you are standing on the precipice of this discovery. You will soon know the blossoming of this knowing in your heart and soul. Rejoice in the wonderment of it all. Allow life to unfold and feel the love that surrounds you and is in you. This is the beginning and the end of each project, of each day, of each thought. With this knowledge and delight in you, you will feel all you need to know and see all you need to see. You will find true happiness in your life and in the lives of others.

Play in the realm of the Almighty and you will find whatever you need to know and learn. You will know the love of God and that the sustenance and happiness you crave is within you and around you at all times. You will forever be held in its bounty. This is the blessing of the Lord of Hosts and the blessing of all who enter the Kingdom of Heaven.

Heaven is in your heart, and your heart is the heart and soul of God. Do not ask what you must do. Allow your heart and soul to open to the love of God and all that exists. Open to the love of the eternal and allow it to flow through you. This is your mission. Fulfill it and you will know the happiness and fulfillment of the saints. You will be enlightened to the hearts and souls of all.

The spirit of the being known as Gabriel

Time-space Continuum

You may have periods in your life when you are absorbed in fantasies and dreams. This may be frustrating, as it seems that you are off of your path. For now, let us set aside judgments on how you spend your time and look at the time-space continuum. You may worry that you are losing your mind lost in daydreams. Yet what you do is create a reality from your dreams—your "escape" from reality.

What if reality is not just your work and what you do materially in the world? What if your daydreams are as much a part of your reality as your material works? Have you noticed that what you dream you can create? You are mastering this art when you ask the Creator for something. You know how to create by asking for something. You visualize it, or think about it, then ask God for it—and it happens for you. This seems remarkable only if you believe that you are creating miracles. What you are doing, however, is merely tapping into the way life miraculously works.

There is much to be done in the world, and much more that is possible. We observe you creating great works of art; we see others creating delicious food dishes, interesting movies, successful business deals, and wonderful communications. This is not done through material work. This is all done through creative insight and evaluation on a higher level. The actual work is done in the material, but the planning and creation is done when you dream.

It is complicated when you dream about relationships and people in your life. This is even more complicated because you are not actually creating for the future here. You are communicating and co-creating dreams with the other person. The dreams you have with others are akin to the astral travel you do on the dream planes of sleep. You are actually dreaming during the day, and it seems that you are clearing the way for more important matters when you release these dreams. What you are doing is clearing the way for appropriate relations by clearing up old karma, images, and ways of relating that do or do not work in the present.

If you dream of having an affair with a man, you are creating it with him at some level. You can actually have this "affair" for a long period of time. Many people have these dream affairs for years and even lifetimes. They are as real as matters on the earth plane, and in these affairs you work out karma, learn new things, share information, and seek pleasure or pain. Yes, some of you enjoy painful dreams because you continue to have and support them. Better that you have them on the dream level than in reality. Furthermore, you can release the fears you've had of relationships or other such matters by playing out alternatives on the astral dream plane. It is very simple and very effective.

Now take your time hearing this because it is important to remember. You are not creating all of your dreams in what you call "real" life. You are not creating a manifestation on the physical unless you ask for it. Remember how you create? Visualize what you want and then ask for it. If you are dreaming, you are visualizing. If you do not ask for it, it will not happen.

This is very effective for people who are too afraid to have a relationship on the physical plane, or who are previously committed. These people can live a life on another level while experiencing life on the material level. If the dream life becomes too involved, it can take over the physical life. This is not usually the optimal use of a body, though some have chosen to do this. You can see them on street corners, in mental institutions, or sometimes sitting in front of a television set for hours.

I once observed a boy who would sit on the couch staring into the room, unseeing. He'd sit there for hours. He seemed unproductive, wasting his time on a couch all day doing nothing. But he was not doing "nothing." The boy was actually creating worlds in his dreams. He was rarely in the material world; and it was not surprising that the boy died a few weeks later. He left to pursue his dreams and creations, his follies on the astral dream world. His spirit then could create without having to manifest or care for a body, which he no longer wanted to do.

It's all very simple, really. Some things take more time than others and need to be manifested in real matter to be seen. For example, take the creation of a sculpture. It looks great in the dream state, but the creation of it in clay is an entirely different matter. Many issues come up in the clay that you would not have foreseen. The way the clay moves and how your hands move with it, the structure of the clay itself and the history it has lived—these are all a part of the experience of sculpting. Creating pretty pictures in your mind is creative and fun. Creating them in matter is growth-producing at an entirely different level, combined with extraordinary complications and events.

It is fair to blame yourself when you waste an entire day in daydreams like the boy did. It is a waste of a body to continually daydream, but is sometimes necessary. For instance, daydreaming is effective when you are mourning a great loss. When you mourn, you remember times with the loved one. You also live out scenarios that you could have shared. Then you are also reliving your dreams with this person and you are recreating them together, as the deceased is still in spirit. This process can go on for years. It's an important part of the loss and recovery process. You can actually dream what the other would do in a situation, such as how to raise a child or take care of some property that you both owned. You can have conversations with the person and wind down the relationship and the events or business that you shared. It is quite practical and takes more time in the beginning.

This is not just true of mourning. It's also true when you are creating a new life or a project. For example, a graphic designer may be creating a logo. She spends a lot of time "thinking" about it—actually dreaming about the logo and creating it in her head. It is quite difficult to create a logo, or any art, without seeing it first in this state.

The same is true when creating other aspects of your life. Let's say you want to travel and have a relationship with someone. You imagine it and try it on. You picture what your life would be like when you travel. You are sorting through the experiences of your life with your future projections. It is quite simple and easy to see how daydreaming complicates matters when it is not honored and people are not allowed time to create in this way. Without the playing out of scenarios beforehand in your mind, you are forced to play them out in the material plane only. This is time-consuming and a waste of body time. You can create on the dream plane and see the results of your actions. Then you can see how the scenario will turn out and amend your plan in the material realm.

You know that others often confront you on the dream plane. You are asked questions, solicited, seduced, and even lied to. You learn to see that the people in spirit on the astral are not as they are in body. A man may want to play with you on the astral, but in reality—on the material plane—he is not available. This is time-consuming. You may want to release those who do not do you justice. You may not have dream time to play with everyone. It is best to be selective.

It may be time to reconsider what you want to do with your life, and this takes time. You are reorganizing theelements of your life and rebalancing your environment so that you can have a new life. This takes dream time. You still need to bring in new people and income. But you are not wasting time when you dream. You are not slowing down your growth and the movement of your life when you have a lot less happening for you. Instead you are relying on your instincts to take advantage of this time in a new, creative, and profitable way. You are learning to dream effectively. Is this not your wish? Use this time; use the skills you learn in your daydreams. Bring the information and the energy into your life, and the knowledge will catapult you into a new arena much faster than you could imagine.

The spirit of the being known as Jesus

God-self and Ego—I

L et's discuss the relationship with the Higher Self. First of all, let me note that it is not actually higher or lower. It is Self. It is one and the same in all its forms. You may look at a part of it and differentiate it from the whole, making it godlike and then worshipping it. True, it is important to listen to this Higher Self. We'll call it God-self, as it's closest to God when you are in body.

Let's begin with the relationship between the God-self and the ego. You may want to rate the God-self as superior to the ego. Many have given supreme examples of how the ego is harmful and challenging to the God-self. This is not true. In fact, the ego is essential in order for one to live on the earth plane. It's important to have an ego to interpret reality in the body and to respond appropriately. It is not sufficient to have a body. The body needs a personality and a means of projecting the energy force to others on the planet. Your ego has that role and can do a remarkable job if trained properly.

The unfortunate aspect of this scenario is that many have

untrained egos. Untrained egos are like wild horses that go where they please and lead no one. A wild horse is beautiful in the wilderness, but is of no use to humans. Humans need to interact in a civil and loving way. Horses learn to behave in order to talk to humans, or to be lead by them. Humans need the same training from birth on.

Children are adorable and loving when born, but they can learn behaviors around them that lead them to do things not worthy of humans. These behaviors are the result of improperly trained egos. You can take an ego and show it many things, but you must never allow it to have control of your faculties. When the ego is in control, it will destroy your life and often your body. It will respond only as it can, with the personality of an animal. You can train the animal to behave appropriately, but only if you are training it with a wise and loving heart. Animals who are trained by hatred, bigotry, and fear respond in kind. They become hating, bigoted, and fearful. Therefore, many learn to mistrust the ego because it has been wrongly trained.

There is a way to remedy this situation. Allow the God-self to train or retrain the ego. Here is where you are not open to the advice of others. It is important that your Higher Self do the training here, as you are building an ego structure that warrants being the vessel of the God-self, and is at one with it. You cannot create an ego that follows the lineage of another and then expect your soul to house itself fully in it. There will be an incompatibility there.

This is important to note when raising a child. It's important to teach the child appropriate manners and ways of speaking. When a child's personality is attacked and molded, however, you are making it difficult for the child to carry on without strife. There will not be a full blending of the two parts, and the child is apt to do and say things he/she doesn't mean. Later in life it's impossible to lead a life of the soul, as the soul is unable to communicate fully with its ego. It's similar to you attempting to talk to the birds. With mild conversations and nuances, you can warn each other, honor each other, and say hello, but you cannot know what it is to be a bird. Unless the ego is open and available to the soul, it is not capable of finding it and honoring it. The soul does not have a proper launching pad.

Much of the work of those on a spiritual path is to train the ego to be accepting and to honor the Higher Self. It often takes years of releasing hatred, pain, and the opinions and beliefs of others. Even those who are in power will often not know themselves. They are not in touch with their higher nature because they are not aware of it in ego. The ego then becomes a block to the yearnings of the soul instead of an asset in the soul's creation of reality to suit itself. To change this entirely often requires years of work, and then the most profoundly difficult work is letting go of past patterns and beliefs, and the life that forms itself around such.

An article was written recently about men who had succeeded because they were not given enough love when they were children. They then began to seek fame and fortune to fill the hole left by abandonment. This is not uncommon. It is important in the lives of all people who are here on Earth that they be given love in great measure. However, this often does not happen and what results is a loveless ego.

This ego is very difficult to reach because it feels unsupported. It then becomes terribly self-sufficient in order to solve its problems and heal its wounds. This is a tragedy to some because they cannot break the pattern for fear of abandonment or being hurt. There is always the opportunity and the necessity of reaching this Self in order to progress appropriately.

Many people bang around in life trying this or that and never reach their Higher Self. This is not important for some. They think that what they have or know on the material plane is all there is. But when the rewards of the Earth are over, the body leaves and the spirit is left with nothing but a collection of unfulfilling or unhealthy experiences.

It's not necessary to experience the negative, the release from God, the untrue and untoward side of life. It's healthy to seek and find your true self, when you're ready to make a change in your life. But if you find and become your true self, your material life may not improve. You may be surprised. The God-self may not want a life of material and business success. It may want to take a break, relax and enjoy the experience of life in a body. You may find that you quit your job or even change careers. Finding your true path may mean staying where you are in life and finding ways to enjoy yourself more. Or, you may have to change direction and find yourself another reality altogether. Fortunately, whatever your role, you will be all the happier being you in entirety—fulfilled in destiny.

It's not unusual for people to quit their jobs when they "find" God. It's unfortunate, though, when they "find" God and think that God is the only answer to all their problems. God is the answer; but God is also the question, and YOU are the answer. If you trust in God and give nothing of yourself, you will get only questions. God and you are connected through spirit, which will lead you along God's path. It is through spirit that you'll see the light you must follow. Your spirit is in touch with the God Source and will be able to guide you to the light. It is here that you will learn to follow your heart and trust yourself to make decisions and answer the call of Life. You are never wrong when you make a decision because you may learn from whatever decision you make.

Let's look at a scenario: You are born with an agenda to do specific things in life. You accomplish everything in exactly the correct way, making no mistakes, living a full life, and arriving at your destination. What then? You'll be terribly bored. Why? Because you've learned nothing. You've taken on only what you can handle and have lead a safe life—safe from harm, hurt, and distraction; safe from fulfillment, overwhelming joy, targeted emotional passion, and hunger for another's love. Great tragedy begets great love, and vice versa.

It is the same defensive strategy when you live only for the moment. You are ready to fulfill your destiny and your dreams reach new and more intensely vibrant dimensions. You will soar, as you now know the folly of not taming your ego. Your personality and ego will sing, and you will now be radiating the spirit of who you are entirely. You will find your path laden with the gold of truth, and your heart filled with the love of all. This is the greatest gift. You will find it so and will never turn back.

Once you've lived a life aware of being a soul in a body, you will know what it's like to remember your Self. When you do, you'll see yourself as a mirror, and the true light will shine on forever because one that knows his own creation, or the bringing of light into form, knows that he/she can exist forever. When you're not in body you can maintain that same recollection and connection to your Self. You will be whole and will remain so in the afterlife.

The spirit of the being known as Jesus

God-self and Ego—II

The ego is a precious commodity indeed. The fact that it's organic makes it untamable if treated like an ornament, and impossible if treated like a king. If the ego has ruled throughout one's life, it is most difficult to force it into submission. The only way to harness such a power is to bring in one that is even greater. That is your Higher Self.

You can bring yourself into the body, and then there is no power greater than you in your own realm. It is you who will judge yourself; you who will end your suffering; you who will delete the harshness from your life. You will create the reality you desire, and you will bring in advisors to help you. It is most important, however, that you know who you are and that you release all ties to those who would control you without the need to know you themselves. You are not a toy to be manipulated, nor are you a pawn in some alien game. You are a human and that is a gift indeed. Your spirit must know to come into the human form and release all obligations other than that—to perform the necessary duties while you're in a body. That is important or else you will take yourself out of the game, and the game will continue without you. You will then have to pay the consequences for allowing your body and ego to run themselves without guidance.

"Come here and look at what I'm showing you." That is a phrase that attracts most people. That will get you in trouble if you do it by leaving your body and going over to where the person is. Most people will question whether they actually leave their body in spirit. It is apparent when you're forgetful or lose things, or if you are daydreaming while doing other tasks. You are focusing somewhere else and not finding the answers from within. "Within" is within you and within the body.

You need the energy of the body to steer you correctly on this journey on Earth. You also need the energy of your Higher Self to steer you and get you on the correct path. If you are not in your body, you are not in touch with the reality of life on the planet and cannot manifest appropriately or correctly.

To some the body seems small and dense compared to the vast lightness of spirit. But a master of the body is in tune with itself. It is not concerned with the tenseness, nor is it concerned with the size. There is no time or space in spirit. Nor is there a need for time and space of spirit in a body. Feel yourself inside of it in spirit. This is not hard. If you try to run the body with spirit, you will fail. The body has its own mechanisms for running itself. You do not want to interfere with these unless you need a healing of some sort. You are not in body when you are traveling on the astral or dreaming. This dreaming serves a purpose when noticed and directed. It is not safe when you're interacting with others, nor out and about in the world. Day-dreaming while driving a car, for instance, is very dangerous. As a spirit you lend insight to the body. You give it direction. You sense and know things that it does not. This information is from other levels. The body needs this information from you and all you need to do is to bring spirit into body.

You are in your body when you do things you enjoy. If you daydream too often, you are escaping. If you escape, you are not living your life and are not accomplishing your life's purpose and journey.

You are not fixed to any place or time. You can move around the planet as you wish. You can live anywhere you choose and do what you like. There are things you must consider, such as income and environment of your family; but you need not tarry on such matters. You will provide for yourself if you are in your body and taking care of yourself accordingly.

It is not unlike times when you are soaring around the dream world. When you are in body you can manifest almost as profoundly as when you are dreaming. You can learn to manipulate your own reality as you see fit. That is not a sin. It is perfectly common and ordinary to change your life to please yourself. It is what God wants you to do. It is your destiny.

If you do things that are inappropriate and know in your heart that you are unhappy, or lying, or partaking in some criminal act, you are not in your body. You are allowing your ego to send you into contests that are not appropriate. You need to be present to run the show appropriately.

The spirit of the being known as Jesus

Aspects of the Human Form

The time you spend in repose and introspection is not wasted time, but magnifies your productivity when you are actually producing. You are not wasting your time when you talk to angels or when you talk to yourself. It is essential and must be accounted for. You must consult your Higher Self and dream of things to come, or you will wear the machine down doing useless work.

Moses lived to 103. Do you think he was running around his whole life? No, he spent most of his time in prayer and contemplation. Look at all he accomplished and how far his deeds have spread.

When you plan a new life or a new day you are being still while the plans are being contemplated and prepared. You are not wasting time—you are creating it. Take time each day for this and you will find that your life moves much smoother. You will see that much gets accomplished while you are meditating. It's not a passive activity. It's actually quite important to the creative process.

We've been speaking about the connections between the different aspects of the human form. There are several bodies that need to be understood to be able to function correctly and appropriately. First you must realize that the astral bodies are actually three in number. There are different aspects to the astral, just as there are to the body. There is emotional, intellectual, and physical (or energetic) in the astral. These aspects comprise the entirety and are essential to the functioning of all of the bodies, including human. The reflection of the human body is seen in the astral, and vice versa. It's possible to see the initial emotions form in one body and travel to the next.

Look at this in yourself. You have suspicions in your emotional body and then you are awakened in the night by dreams that are emotional in nature. Your physical body is not dreaming. Your astral body is. The emotional aspect of the body is reacting to the traumas in the body.

The same effect occurs from the other direction. There are various aspects to the soul-self known as intuitive bodies. These bodies aren't divided into intellectual, emotional, and energetic. Instead they are colored into different spectrums that radiate light of different vibrations. Each vibration houses a different form of energy, which is then shadowed down through to the physical body. This is the natural form of radiation. It is very healing to the astral bodies if it is in sync with the physical body. In other words, when the Higher Self is in tune with the body, it is able to radiate energy that feeds both it and the astral bodies.

Conflict occurs when the body is not in touch with the Higher Self. There's a feeling of overwhelming confusion. It's not healthy for you to have your physical body, astral, and spirit vibrating at different vibrations. That's why it's so important to attune yourself to your Higher Self. An attuned master will allow the Higher Self to fuel the physical body and heal it. The astral travels will be immensely important and will take on an entirely new function in this situation—similar to exploration. The astral will explore for you areas you are not in touch with on either the physical or higher planes.

The spirit of the being known as Raphael

Knowing the God Source Within

I am Raphael and would like to discuss a question that has plagued men and women for centuries, even millenniums. You question how to know and work with the Will of God and decipher it from other sources. It is not a simple one to answer. It could take hours of writing, or I could simply say this: God is with you and in you always. Look for the God in you and you will speak and act the Will of God.

The search for God is a lengthy one. God is everywhere, so where can you look to find God? You look at religion and find God there, but for many it's not the God of their hearts. You look in books and find the Word of God, but this does not bring it into your heart. God is in your heart, speaks the truth for you, and has the answers to all of your questions. This is your truth, just as the God of the heart is the truth for each and every man and woman.

God speaks to you from your heart, and it is here that you hear wisdom and truth. It is here that you receive information and judgment. It is here that you are supported and know the love of God. It is here that you learn to spread that love to others. God is not apart from you. God is in you. Do you see this?

The God of your heart is not a solid entity. People want so much to crystallize everything and pin it down so they can have it, and tame it, and own it. This is true of everything from the material to the wishes of the heart. But life isn't like that. The love of your heart is not a stagnant entity that has one truth and one answer.

I know you want a pillar to stand on, a podium to cling to; but there is no right or wrong that does not change in time. There is no direction that doesn't move and shift. Everything in the universe is shifting and altering its course. This is also true of humans. You want a steady-state answer, but you'll find that your heart is fickle. It changes. You change.

So now you wonder whom to trust. Who better than the God of your heart? It is true that the heart changes and shifts. It grows and changes with you. So your answers are, at best, current. It is not for you to ask or remain unfaithful. It is not for you to doubt. It is true that as you grow, your heart grows; you are one entity and you will grow together. Your heart, your ego, and your body will all learn to act together. Your heart will guide you. Your mind will persuade you and consider. Your body will carry you and manifest in the energy fields that surround you. It is in this present state that you will begin to create a new reality.

From your heart you will speak the truth. From your heart you will know the truth. From your heart you will live the truth and know that it is an honor to be present on the planet. With this vehicle called a body, you are able to fully grow and shift yourself in spirit. It is not an easy journey to take. You are not just looking to fulfill yourself. You are asking to fulfill your soul purpose. The true indicator of where you need to go next is your heart.

How do you find the God within? You do not have to access this part of yourself. It is there. You only need to become open to it and allow yourself expression of it. It is not hard to do. You know your heart better than anyone does. It is the voice that speaks to you when you're tired and need sleep. It is the feeling that you have when you see a sunset. It is the warmth and lovingness you feel when you are looking at someone you love. The heart is the true indicator and barometer of the soul.

To honor yourself you need only respect this part of yourself and honor it with truth and appropriate response. The heart may not speak to you directly. You may not hear words or see miracles in front of your eyes. Your heart speaks in a subtle manner. It talks to you in your head when you are least expecting it. It is the voice you hear when you're angry. It is the "conscience" you imagine when you are missing something or behaving inappropriately. The heart is the key indicator of your every want and desire, and your inner voice of truth.

.

The spirit of the being known as Gabriel

Surrender and Control

I am Gabriel, and I'd like to talk to you about the concepts of control of your life and surrendering to life. Control is not an issue to be dealt with. It is an illusionary concept that the ego uses to think that it is making things happen. There is no control at the ego level. In fact, there is no control at ANY level, nor is there any type of surrender or "victimhood." The true state of attunement is not bewildering. It is quite simple actually: Know that everything is being created in the moment and that you are on a path of creation. You are the spearhead of the God-force as it makes its way into creation. You manifest the Creator as the impulse runs through you.

One dilemma is that you feel you have to be present in time. You are certain that knowing the schedule of your next days will ascertain a happy, productive time. This is not always true. To allow God to take the helm means knowing that everything is happening as it needs to. You may not plan far in advance, but your Higher Self knows what needs to happen on the earth plane and on other levels. When you try to create and plan from the ego level, you get only strife. The ego is not meant to run the show. The ego is meant to live and play among others, and to be in touch with the other parts of life that you can't access now. The ego is banned from moving outside of the body.

There is a belief that you can make things happen from the earth level. In truth, you cannot. All that occurs is planned before it reaches the body level–worked through at other levels of reality, and manifested on the earth plane. True, it appears that the actions are occurring and are enacted from the human plane, but this is an ego perception. If you look deeper, you'll see that you can be more aware of what is occurring at all levels. Your ego may want to change a situation at the earth level and may have a fit trying to make something happen. It's like a 2-year-old child throwing a temper tantrum when he can't have his way. The ego's way is to have everything planned and carried out according to plan. This is not the optimal state of existence. All that happens is predetermined and will not conform to the whims and expectations of the ego. This is difficult for the ego to understand and much more difficult for the ego to accept. It is your choice whether you act like the 2-year-old or learn to trust your Higher Self.

Your Higher Self knows what to do. Trust it. Right now you know what you need to do. Will you feel more comfortable if you know now what you'll do next? Who is more comfortable if you know the plan? How can you plan for tomorrow if you are not being present in the now? Now you cannot plan for tomorrow because tomorrow is not clear. It will be clear soon. If you trust, you will find that you have plenty of time to make. You will know the answers in time—in enough time—to make your decisions and plans.

This is a new way of working for many of you. You want to have a plan to stick to. Then you are upset when you have interruptions to your plan. For example, you may plan to work today on a project, but you do not feel inspired to work. If you force yourself, your time will be unproductive. If you stay present you will see what is truly best for you to accomplish now. Then when it is time, your project will come together perfectly.

You cannot tame the ego. It is not a being that grows as the soul does. It will not alter its course and become like the soul. The ego is meant to play and interact with others. It is not meant to control or take charge of your life in any way. If you give it the opportunity, it will cause much strife and discontent in your life. The easiest way to understand and control the ego from the Higher Source is to allow the ego to voice its complaint and then answer it like you would a child. You can appreciate the strife and stress that the ego undergoes. Acknowledge it and honor it. Then tell the ego that you will take care of whatever situation it's concerned about.

You make a plan from your Higher Self and tell your ego what you intend. You could say something like, "I'm just going to enjoy myself now and work on the project later in the day. That will be my decision for now." Do you see the relief? You are released from the plan.

The spirit of the being known as Mary

Relationships

I am the one you call Mother Nature. I am the one you know as the Goddess. I am also known as Mary and in some circles, Josephine. I am the heart and soul of the entity you know as God. The God Source is neither male nor female. I am one part of the God Source that is known as the Mother, the Father, and the Holy Spirit. You will know the trinity and the creative forces of all creation through the forces that create these. You are not free until you know the love of the female in yourself. It is the heart of the Mother that lives in everyone. I speak to you from that place, although you see it as foreign because you have only spoken to the part you see as male.

I would like to answer a question that is in the heart of many—the question of how to love and not lose oneself in the relationship. The question is not, "How do I love and not lose myself?" The real question that sits in the heart of everyone is, "How do I stay aligned with my God-self and not lose myself to another person?"

You want to fulfill your purpose on Earth, yet may have

often lost track of your own needs and sacrificed yourself for the needs of others. It is not wrong to give and to support someone. It is appropriate to help others and to be supportive. Yet there is a time when you feel yourself being bled from an energetic standpoint.

It is a very deep and sacred spot, this heart you dream of. It is at the root and core of everything you want to tap into. It's easy and natural to believe that you can tap into this by feeding another. You then begin to look at the other as the source of this love. If you do not get the love from another, you feel you are lost and are not fulfilling your mission. If you are not with another, you feel that you are not able to tap into this love. The truth, as you suspect, is that the love you seek and wish to share is not in the heart of another, but is in the heart of all life.

You can see this heart in the lives of everyone—in what they do and create. You can see this heart when a man discovers a great secret to the unfolding of a mission he's been on. You can see it in the face of a happy child who has discovered joy in a fun experience. The joy you seek, the intimacy you wish to share, is not in the heart of another. It is in the heart of you. You want to share your own heart with another, not share another's heart. You want to remember your own heart and to live in it— to breathe it and share it with others.

You may believe that it's best to only share your heart with those you trust. It seems safer this way because you've been hurt in the past. But as a child you were open and loving with everyone. At that time the people around you may not have returned the love you gave in full measure. They may have scorned you and disciplined you unnecessarily with harsh words and anger. Perhaps you were scared and you closed off your heart to others, thinking that they would harm the heart and soul of the God-self within you. You protected yourself from the pain that you were experiencing by closing off your heart.

This is a common reaction to pain. It is common to want to escape from reality when you are hurt. The easiest way to do this is to close off your heart because the heart is the doorway and key to the soul. You believe that if you close your heart you will close off the portal that keeps you here, and prevent others from harming you.

This is true to a certain extent, especially if you do not know how to protect yourself. It's natural to a child who loves and is then hurt. The child does not understand the workings of humans. The innocent child does not know the torment in some people's souls and the pain they experience. When confronted by pain and suffering at an early age, it is bewildering and frightening. It leaves a wound that is difficult to repair.

As an adult, you understand more when a person dishonors you with criticism and pain. You know that the person has problems of their own and that it is not your fault when this person is mean to you. You also know to move out of the way of those who are hostile—at least most of the time. As a child, you do not know this and it is frightening.

So how do you love when you've been hurt and closed off for so long? You learn to share parts of yourself with another, but not all of yourself. You divvy out bits and pieces of your love so that you are not hurt. You feel that however much you open up to this person, you can be hurt. There is a feeling that, "If I only open up 'this' much to a person, I can only be hurt 'this' much." The truth is, you are only hurting yourself by closing off the heart. You are basing the relationship on pain from the beginning because you are not allowing your love to flow through you to another. It is doomed to failure because you are only giving what you THINK you should give, and not what you feel or want to give in spirit. The mind then controls the heart and you've set up a pattern for pain. It is an unfortunate circumstance because the mind does not understand the workings of the heart. It understands a great deal, but the mind and heart are of different realms. There is no way that the heart is able to open to the mind when it is controlled by it. It is the heart that has to rule itself and be its own taskmaster, its own savior, its own light.

Let's look at what you have created in your life. Perhaps you have friends, animals, and people in your life who love you, yet you feel that there is still a lack. You want to know the true intimacy that comes from a deep and meaningful relationship. You want to be able to share your deepest feelings with another, but not be hurt by this person. You want to know the love of the Divine in a relationship with another, but not get lost in this relationship. This is a natural and meaningful goal.

You want a man or woman to fulfill you. It is not possible to be fulfilled by another; consequently, many people are helplessly lost in relationships. It is sad when a loving person gives what little heart there is to give and is rejected—often closing off even that small part of the heart. It is also difficult to see someone who wants to love and doesn't know how because there is so much pain blocking the transmission of love.

People often come together to share love in order to be

reminded of the love they have in themselves. The love you are seeking is in yourself, of course. You've heard this and it's been written of many times before. Still, it is not understood because people do not see this love in themselves; they only see it in others. They use others as a mirror of their own love. When the mirror reflects pain, as it often does, it is difficult to look at.

So the next step is to attempt to change the person you are attempting to love (and be loved by) so that they will display the love you want to receive. It is not essential that the person love you in the way you desire. It is just important that the actions they exhibit show you the love you are seeking. If they do not show you this love, you feel they are lacking—or you are lacking. It is felt that a lack of love from another is just an abnormality in the other or in the relationship. It is not realized that the lack of love, in reality, is due to the pain that is being harbored in you in place of the love.

So what you have is an endless circle of pain and ineffectual attempts to discover real love. For example, let's say there is a woman who wants to be cherished, but is receiving only ridicule. She sees this ridicule as a reflection and wants to change this reflection to be more loving. She will either become angry with her mate or with herself (or both) because the love is not coming through to her. She will then try to alter herself or her mate to become more loving. The situation will be manipulated until the love that is surrounding her is displayed in her mate.

At times, this method actually works. People get together and wear each other down enough where they must open their hearts to experience the love. Once the battle is won, and the ego is defeated and lying bloodied on the floor, the heart opens and love is found. They think this loving is due to the other, and so they become dependent on the other for this love. It is the case with most couples when they build a life of love between them and do not share this love with others. Of course, we're talking only of love of the heart.

It is natural to seek a mate who will give you the freedom to love and yet be yourself. You want to know what it is like to love so deeply that you are not afraid to open your heart and share with another. There are others in your life who love you; you see this and reflect it. It is a beautiful sight to behold. The fallacy comes when you believe that this is the only place you can receive this love. You think that you need this person to feel it. What if you take the love you feel, this love that is reflected in you, and savor it without identifying it with the other person?

Realize that the love you share with one person is not an end, but is a catalyst for you to open your heart to love everyone. Then you can begin to look for love in everyone and not be disappointed when you don't find it. Although there is love in everyone, some people protect it quite well and it is difficult to see. If you are strong in your love, you will have the strength to find the love in others. This is a key to helping them open to their own hearts and to the heart of the God Source. It would be giving them a great gift.

Now you see the beauty and value of a relationship that does not bind you. You can be with a person who knows the freedom of being all that he is, and still have your own freedom to share your love with others. You can use the relationship as a tool to rediscover the love in yourself. But remember that lack of love is not a lack of loving in the person. It is the inability to open the heart from the pain that is experienced. Whenever you encounter a lack of love in your mate, it is not you that he is failing to love, but himself. Have compassion. Do not fear the lack of love. Love your way through this fear and you will find the light of the God Source is in you at all times. Then the relationship takes on new meaning.

Soon you will see life as an opportunity to open your heart and love in the midst of great fear and suffering in the world. It is a great accomplishment to be able to love in human form. It is easier on the angelic realm and in the astral; but in body you feel the pain of others and yourself.

You know the pain of lack of love. With others you are unaware of the great strides that are taken to love you and therefore you are not as certain of the love that is around you at all times. Seek to find this love. When you remember that the love in your heart is also a reflection of the love that is in and around you at all times, you will know the love of God. Here is when the true beauty unfolds and you are able to see the love in all things. You will see that love is forever in you and around you. You will know that you are blessed at all times, no matter the pain.

The opportunities to feel and reinforce the love of God are numerous. Each time you feel pain and open your heart to it, you heal a wound in yourself and in the God Source. Each time you know in your heart that you are one with the Creator and are free to love, you heal the wounds of centuries. You are the source of the love. When you feel this love in and around you, you will radiate it and show others the beauty of all creation.

Now the true goal is manifested. Now you begin the journey of unfolding, as you become the source and the messenger of love for the Creator. Now you see that all people are children, including yourself. You are all the children of God spreading the message of God through love.

The lack of love is not a lack of God, but rather the inability to express love because of pain. If you find another who helps you and allows you to open your heart, treasure this relationship. Do not hold onto it or attempt to change it. Do not be disappointed when the other person can't love you in the moment. Remember instead the love that you know in you, and radiate it.

No, this is not an easy task. It is not easy to be human. It is the life's work of many, and the job is never ending. For when you learn to expand into the Life Force, you see that the Life Force is expanding in you. Then the true creation begins.

The spirit of the being known as Buddha

Expectations vs. Dreams and Intentions

Sometimes we look too far for the love we cherish. We look to others for the love and appreciation we feel we lack. It is not an inappropriate request to want to be adored. However, it is not appropriate to demand or even request it from others.

It is not wrong to move out of the way of other people's pain. In fact, it is preferable. If you let them continue to be irritated by your presence, you are adding to your own pain as well as theirs. You begin to see that you are learning to nurture and love yourself. You will attract people into your life who also feel the same about themselves.

When you do not love or appreciate yourself, you attract people who feel the pain of not being loved and appreciated by themselves. This is because you do not fully love. You will bring pain into your life with these people. You cannot shut people out of your life, nor should you. But, you can take the time to heal and love yourself when you need it.

So many look to others for solace and love. It is not possible to be healed by others. It is only possible to be healed by yourself. It is not possible to completely fit into anyone else's life agenda. If you do, you will be lost with no identity and nothing to offer life. People who do attempt to fit into others' agendas feel neglected and hurt. If you ask for help, you are seen as a burden. If you state your needs, you are seen as being out of order. You have needs, but they are not often accounted for in the plans of others—and there is really no way they could have been. Others do not know your needs. You only know what you need. When you see that your needs are not being met, you accommodate yourself.

Having no expectations is a key to happiness. With expectations, you plan your day outside of the flow of reality. With dreams and intentions, you set the pace for the energy you desire. Without this you see only the pace of others and are not set in the ways of the world.

The spirit of the being known as Gabriel

The Creative Process

L et's look at the creative process. To create a dream, you first have one. In other words, you imagine what it is you want— how you'd like your life to progress. You visualize it and then ask the Universe (with your intention) to provide it for you. From that point on you will receive information from your Higher Self, your ego, and from others to complete your goals. If you listen, follow these instructions, and act on the opportunities given to you—and do not change your dream midstream—you will attain your goal and your dream will come true.

This is different from manipulating the energy to attain your goals. If you dream a goal and then manipulate events to achieve it, you are working from ego and are acting against the flow of the natural order. When you do this, you are creating confusion in the energy fields, which causes repercussions. This often happens when people lie or cheat to become famous, rich, or popular.

For example, when a person has a goal and then knowingly hurts others to achieve it, he is altering the energy of others in ways that are not productive. The energy may move in his favor for a short period of time—maybe even a lifetime, though this is rare. Eventually the manipulations will cause havoc in the order and there will be an extreme adjustment, causing the initiator great pain. Some call this karma; others call it justice. Either way, it's merely a righting of the energies to the original and necessary order.

Do you see the difference? One way is allowing the Universe to create and help you create. The other way is attempting to alter and change the Universe for your own aims and ideals. One person cannot alter the flow for long. It's akin to being in a large rubber band. If you move and force the rubber in one direction, you may see some changes occurring in your space. However, the rubber will right itself. If you pull it and deform it too much, it will pop back in a way that is very unpleasant and even painful. Sometimes it will harm you to the extent that it actually affects the physical realm and your body will be altered. This is not common. Do not confuse this with body changes that occur because of the natural order; but there are times when justice is harsh because the force WILL be restored.

You've most likely seen the effects of moving too quickly toward your aim. You've seen how you can ask for something and then try to manipulate the situation to suit what you think is your ideal. You may try to act appropriately and are not aware of manipulating the situation. Or, you may be acting in fear.

There is a tendency to observe fear as an indicator of the truth. It is not. Fear is an indicator to look more closely at the situation. Often the lesson or information you find is not based upon the fear that you feel. You may fear that a person will harm you. When you look closer, you'll learn that you are in danger of hurting yourself. The lesson is there, but the fear is not necessarily pointing to the truth in the situation. Fear is an indicator, not an aberrant message.

Let's look at an example where you are involved in a business transaction that is taking a negative turn. You are in fear of losing the transaction because you feel taken advantage of. Perhaps your associate acts in anger and you react to this anger with fear. You are certain that this associate is going to undermine you and take advantage of you. This leaves you emotionally drained and exhausted on many levels. You project this fear onto the situation and then act in a manner that assures your survival, though you may sacrifice the transaction. You do not see the situation clearly.

Here is the associate's perspective. He is in a great deal of emotional pain and is feeling tremendous stress from it. He is not upset with you, but feels out of control in his own life and lashes out at you in anger. You can see his actions as symptoms of a man in great pain. You can see his anger as an attempt to bail himself out. Instead you take his gyrations personally and are hurt by them, and then respond in a manner that ends the deal.

This happens often in life. People assume that others who act in anger and pain are reacting to them. They assume that this anger and pain, and the resulting repercussions, are symptoms of their own lives. This usually is not the case. The anger, pain, and actions are merely reactions to the incidents in the individual who is expressing them. You were merely in the way.

Next time get out of the way of those who are stressed

beyond control. They will only hurt you. Do not try to heal them or teach them. There is little to be learned when a person is overly stressed or extremely tired. There is little healing that can be had. Allow the person to come to terms with his or her own lessons and events. Then be there for comfort or information when and/if he or she asks for it. It is not your job to remain in the eye of someone else's hurricane. Get out of the storm before your house is destroyed.

Here's another lesson. You may encounter people who live in an intensely off-balance reality, such as someone who plans his life according to the needs and whims of others. A person who is constantly trying to please others has little time for himself. He is completely out of sync with reality because he is out of sync with his own needs.

You will see what happens when a person tries to accomplish too much, most of which is based on the needs of others. This man may be a caring person who wants to help others. He may devote his life to it. However, he is not healing himself. He has allowed the needs of others to control him. Here is a situation when the rubber reality bends in the opposite direction. This man has allowed the manipulations of others to bend his own reality. This reality will snap back, and if you're in the way you will be hit by his pain.

So you see that to be in pain you need only honor the needs of others above your own, and/or try to honor your own needs above others and manipulate reality to suit those needs. In either case, you have the same result—pain.

Look at the life you are creating around you. Do not stare at the pain and the repercussions of the lessons you're learning.

Instead focus on the creation you have manifested and on the dreams you intend for the future. The lessons will heal and you will learn from them. You will not have to manipulate the situation so that you learn from the experience. Intend that you will learn and it will happen. Now let go of the experience and move on to a more pleasant situation.

The spirit of the being known as Mary

Feminine Energy; Love

I'd like to discuss the role of the feminine. If you are in a female body, you see eye to eye with another female in a way that you do not with a man. You are a woman in form and radiate the feminine energy. When you speak to a male entity, he seems different from you. A female voice seems to come from within. It is very close. The feminine voice and energy is a part of all of us, particularly those in women's bodies. For them this energy is difficult to define and almost impossible to defend because it seems to be a part of you.

If you are a woman, the voice of all women moves through you. It is like a force field that radiates from the heart and moves through your base chakras, through the womb. The voice of the female comes from the depths of the spirit, in the place that is closest to the Earth's energy, and runs like a brook through your heart.

You are the embodiment of the Holy Spirit as it moves through the spirit of mankind and womankind. This is true of all women. Though the spirit of the holy runs through all and permeates each and every cell and atmospheric particle, the women of mankind know it as their own.

It is here that you resonate from the heart; it is here that you know your God Source; it is here that you know your role; and it is here that you are fighting with confusion. As the Holy Spirit manifests through mankind, it changes form to match and communicate with the Father and the Son.

The Mother brings peace and serenity to the planet and to your souls. The Mother is the nurturer who feeds the soul with love and understanding. This is the origination of peace and serenity. It cannot be achieved without love and understanding of self and soul.

The truth is unveiled by the wisdom of the Mother. It is not a spoken truth, but a truth of knowing. The presence and the knowing are not explainable. There is merely a feeling of wisdom and a depth of oneness that prevails. Through this comes a solidity and power—a force inherent in understanding through the heart of the Mother.

The male voice in us could challenge this truth with words and logic, and it would not be defensible because this wisdom has no words to express it. The source is through the heart and soul. It creates through the womb and expresses itself through the heart. We are the Mother of the God Source, just as we are the Father and are one with God. God is all of these and more. The combination of the three is a power beyond understanding.

You see that there is little to say here, but we are present and need to be heard—to be known. It is important that all embody the spirit of the Mother in heart, so that the growth and development of all will be known.

You may have questions about being receptive and are wondering about control and how women are to behave when with the male. These are very important questions and the answers are being reformulated. The female is emerging in a new form and seeks the respect and admiration that is due. The male is not opposed to this, but does not know how to behave and treat this power. It is confusing to the male energy because the male expression needs form and structure to behave in time.

The female must define the way she wants to be treated. This is not done with violence or harshness, as a male warrior would do. This is done with love, which is the gift and form of the female. It is important to recognize the gifts of the male. The male will provide for the female in a worldly manner. I know these concepts seem outdated, but please bear with me as you learn to see that the male and female reside in everyone. We are talking about concepts and energy here.

The female is broad and far-reaching. She is not as outspoken, but speaks with her heart. She yearns for peace and serenity. She longs for appreciation and support by being loved and cherished. The female love wants to meet the male in mutual attraction and admiration. She does not want to control the male, nor does she want to be controlled. She wants to be appreciated and adored— to be honored for the power that she is.

If a male honors the woman in this way, he is already feeding her and caring for her, as she desires. If he chooses to provide food for her, that is wonderfully accepted. If he wants to take her places and show her things, this is honored as well. It is neither expected nor demanded. The mother demands nothing, she just IS. It is the role of the male to provide and to find ways of entertaining the female, guiding her into areas that she will enjoy. If a male is not guiding well, it is important that the female go elsewhere. It is not useful for the female to be lead into areas or activities that do not allow her peace and serenity. It is important that the Mother's love be allowed full expression. In fact, it is not possible to be or embody the Mother if you are not in a place or activity that will promote this. It is common sense, but too often ignored. You cannot expect to be placed in a situation that is harmful or discordant and still know the love of the Mother within you. This negative energy squelches the energy of the Mother. She must withdraw and find another medium or time to express herself.

This is important to realize. In order for the Mother to find expressions in love and harmony, she must reside in a place and situation of harmonious vibrations. There is nothing more to be said or done with this.

Sometimes people are born into austere conditions, exposed to poverty and abuse. These are situations that promote the growth of the Father. These situations promote warrior tendencies, not loving tendencies. Love will provide a key to open the door to a new way of acting and being. It will not prevail if the conditions do not change. It is not possible.

The way to change this life is to love yourself. Then you will remove yourself from the abusive situation so that you can experience this love, and a new feeling of peace will prevail.

You are not in a serene environment if you are feeling loneliness or unhappiness. If you have these feelings, you need to change something in order to feel the love you desire. This is a key issue. You cannot change the world with love. You can only change the world to allow it. Then love will transform all of you and everything. Loving a murderer will not stop him or her from murdering you. Moving away from the murderer will prevent him from murdering you and will allow you to continue to love. Moving to a new side of town, away from noise and pollution that is harmful to you will create an environment that promotes love and healing. If you cannot move, you can love yourself enough to find a means of changing your environment so that you can experience the full benefit of this loving force.

If you encounter a person who treats you poorly, you can still attempt to radiate love. This will change the atmosphere. If you attempt to change the other person by loving him or her, you are attempting to alter the other. This is not appropriate. If you are trying to remain loving so that you can maintain this feeling in yourself, you are fighting to maintain love in the midst of adversity. However, notice that as you attempt this, you are feeling less love than when you began relating to this person. You can stay and try to fight the fire by loving it, but you will lose the battle. Love does not flourish in an atmosphere of hatred and destruction. Love is a force that fares best when it is given free room to express itself. If you attempt to fight hatred with love, you are becoming the opposite of that which you promote. Love is not meant to be used as a weapon of force. Love is a flower that needs to be allowed room to bloom.

If you are interacting with someone who is harsh or negative to you, and you remove yourself from the situation, you give love room for free expression. If you remain as loving as possible, and continue to interact, you may or may not gain the respect of the person with whom you are doing business. You will gain more respect and teach the person a far more important lesson if you walk away and interact with someone else. You will be saying, "In love, I cannot interact with you when you are hateful." This will allow the love within the other to seek expression, as there is none outside of him. You should love those who are not acting in love, but you need to get out of their way before they destroy the love you feel or want to feel.

Now you see how this speaks to the role of the female. It is quite obvious. You do not need to control the situation. Love does not control and determine how actions will transpire. Love just IS. As a woman, all you need to do is maintain your love by allowing yourself to remain only in situations where others behave lovingly toward you. That is all there is.

Find a way to love yourself, create an environment, and be a person you can love. Do all of these and you will know the force of the Mother. Now digest this for awhile and go love yourself.

The spirit of the being known as Metatron

Manifestation

Many view the Masters as being above them—more knowing and powerful than they are. The extent of your "growth" and ability to be like a Master is your ability to realize that you ARE like one. You are the only being limiting your light, and you do this with your own doubt in yourself. If you do nothing else on Earth, learn to love yourself. For as you do this, you are learning to be yourself and to be the love that you are in the face of God. You are the Almighty and the Almighty is you. You are all angels of God when you realize that you are. And when you don't, you are still the light of the world shining from on high.

I speak in idioms of the past, but I am ancient and do not have the slang of the present to offer you. It is my intent to show all of you that you have much to offer the angels and Masters, as well.

I am a master of manifestation. However, there is an aspect of manifestation that is not recognized. Most people look at manifestation as the culmination of dreams of wealth or happiness. It is true that the final culmination or output of one's intentions is seen as material in the material world; however, there is much more to this process than meets the eye.

Manifestation is not creating something out of nowhere or nothing. Manifestation is the appearance of what has been created in intent and in fullness of being. For example, the other day a woman was lonely and asked that God manifest a date for her for that evening. One hour later she was running errands and saw a man she knew, who asked her out. It may seem that she manifested the date that day. Instead, consider the possibility that she, in soul, wanted and planned the date long before she intended it in ego/body. Perhaps her soul let her in on the secret to let her know to be prepared and ready for the date. That way she thought she created it by asking for it, and was then able to receive it. If the man had showed up without her asking first, she may have turned him down. As it was, she realized that she'd already asked and her prayer was being answered. Pretty manipulative of the soul, you think? Actually you may consider it differently by looking at the power of the soul to manifest and work through her to accomplish her goals.

You think you are here to hone the ego so that it can create, but this is not true. You are much more powerful than you realize. (When I say "you" I am speaking to all who read this.) All souls on Earth are capable of masterful tasks and learning. You are not alone here. You are among billions of remarkable souls. Whether or not you find the need to communicate in the physical is of no consequence. Your world is filled with the light of the souls in it. Bask in it.

Back to manifestation. You see that manifestation is not the intent and the creation from the earth level. It is the intent and mastery of the soul as it manifests through the body. All that you are and all that you have is a manifestation of you in Spirit. You are not the result of aimless wishes. You are the result of a master plan, an intention of life and love that is acting through you.

So now manifestation is not a gambling game where you ask for something and then receive it. It is a project of asking for something and realizing that you are in line with what is being created. You know that you can have what you ask for because you have already intended it in spirit and are now manifesting it by having it appear as an intent on the material plane. You are tapped into this intention whether or not you realize it.

On the other hand, there are times when you feel you've tapped into another type of intention—the intention for evil or negative vibrations. You are unhappy or angry. You ask for things that you know are not self-serving. How does this happen? It occurs when you are tapped into the energy of the planet—the energy of the body and its humanness on the planet—and its manifestation here. The elements of the body are crass compared to the ethers on other planes. They manifest in thoughts that are not purely physical, but have an air of authenticity because they are manifested into physical form. The body has a thought, or chemical, move through it that manifests into physical thought, which is negative. Then you, in spirit, identify with it and think you have negative thoughts.

Let's say, for instance, that you are ill. Your body is hurting and the chemical reactions in it are not up to par with the normal workings of the body. So you lie in bed feeling bad and hurting. You also have thoughts that are bad and hurting. This is common and expected when you are ill. It is not recognized, however, when you are not ill. You might eat something that sets up unsettling chemical reactions in your body, though handled at a level below your pain threshold. These reactions set up thoughts that harm you.

Or, you can also be exposed to negativity in the environment. It is difficult to have positive thoughts when you are subjected to the negative feelings of others who are ill, whether or not it is noticeable. Many reactions and reactives occur in the environment and are picked up by the body. You are not aware of them, but they affect you. They cause negative vibrationsin your body and you manifest them as such. They then tell you things that you don't like to hear. They create negative thoughts.

This is also a form of manifestation. It is a reactive manifestation based upon the environment, both internally and externally. You will create according to that with which you identify. Identify with the patterns and thoughts in the body and you will manifest according to that. Identify with your Higher Self and you will manifest at a Higher Self level—the level of creation that is positive and prosperous.

Recently a documentary aired which told about a well-known athlete. She was raised in poverty in an extremely negative environment. What she did have was love from her family and from a supporting athletic teacher. This is what she identified with and therefore was able to perform miracles.

She also ran and performed great bodily feats while under a tremendous amount of pain. She worked the body until it could no longer work harder. She did not identify with the pain in her body and completed the long jump with an excruciatingly painful hamstring tear. She ignored the pain and instead focused on the intent of her soul. She is a great example of courage and power of intent.

She knew the love in her soul as mirrored by her family and friends. She then was able to manifest this love as a powerful example to others. And what did people on the documentary say about her first? Those who knew her did not say first that she is a great athlete. Instead they spoke of the love that she exudes to others.

So again we get back to the love that is in the hearts and souls of all of us. It is this that manifests for all. It is this that we must tune in to in order to manifest on the physical level. The power of the individual is not how much money he or she makes, or the toys that she or he has. The power is the result of the extent that one is able to connect with the power and intent of the soul. Once you have tapped into your Source, you are on the way to overwhelming security and prosperity of great magnitude.

The spirit of the being known as Mohammed

Healing; Becoming a Peaceful Warrior

Islam is a place in the heart; it is a place where I live. The area of the world I inhabited encompasses or incorporates this place in myself, as well. Do you understand what I'm saying? I'm not as familiar with your language. This English has many more words that all have many meanings.

The people in the region of the world that I inhabited have adopted the essence of my understanding as a religion. This essential soul has permeated the culture and hearts of those who live there.

It is rare to find people outside of Islam who understand my religion. Most who study and practice it stay out of touch with the mainstream of humanity in other regions. Even when they practice the teachings, they choose to share it only with those close to them. This is unfortunate, I think. I wish that my ideas were shared more with everyone. Only humans can truly teach humans. We are all remotely assisting you. We can merely give you advice and learning.

I am no longer human, but I was in human form not long ago.

I came and served in a South American country about 200 years ago. I was able to help and bond with others then. I loved living in the mountains and experiencing the cool mountain air and the streams and woods of the region. Earth is changing much now, but there are still areas such as this. They are precious.

You may know me as a warrior. Do you expect warriors to be harsh and cruel? A true warrior is not one who likes to fight and kill. A warrior is a defender of the truth and the light. A warrior is someone who will defend his (or her, if you wish) beliefs by not being overcome by the ranting and pressure of others.

When one wants to teach of the beauty and love in life, it is important that he/she be allowed to do so. If this is prevented, a space needs to be made for it to happen. Fighting is not something that's acceptable. I hate for this to happen. It is best to be a peaceful warrior, envisioning peace and prosperity among all men and women so that you can practice what you preach and teach.

It is important to be aware of those you are teaching and to only be open to those who open to you. Otherwise you're inviting harshness and strife into your life. If you are a warrior for peace and love, both within yourself and in the world, you will note that you can change only the light of yourself. Then you will alter the flow of humanity's entire destiny with your charm.

The spirit of the being known as Jesus

Criticism and Projection

Today I will give you information about how to handle the complaints and issues of others. The criticisms of others are merely mirrors of what you see in yourself. There is a misconception, however, that what you see in yourself is real and accurate. Listen to me closely. There is no mirror but that which you see in others. There is no other mirror. If you see something in someone else, it is a reflection of what you are inside of you.

There is also a misconception that what you see in others is not you. People project what they see inside of themselves onto others. For instance, perhaps you know a woman who seems loving and fun to you; yet she says that you are harsh and not fun to be around. It's difficult for you to imagine that this woman is mirroring herself onto you and is, herself, harsh and not fun to be around. She seems so light-hearted and entertaining to you. However, this is not the issue. She may be light and entertaining, but SHE does not see herself that way. She is criticizing you based upon what she sees in herself.

You may wonder how people relate to each other at all. If

they are relating based upon what they see in themselves, there is no real communication. People are really reacting to the images they have of themselves and to the responses of others to this.

Let's take the above example further. You could drop the entire conversation and comments from the woman and not take it personally, but believing there is some truth in her words. There is a part of you that bought the entire story that she handed you. Why would you do this? Perhaps you know that people speak of what is mirrored to them, but if this is true, she would be mirroring what she was. You can't see that she is mean and not fun. She doesn't seem that way. So, you conclude that she is correct in her summation of you.

People do not see themselves mirrored in others. People see what they think they are in others. She thinks that she is not fun and is even mean at times. She is afraid that she may channel the energy of meanness, like she sees you doing.

Can you see how this information can be used? Imagine this for a moment. No one sees you for who you really are. Only you see yourself. You can only see yourself by looking at how you see others. If you see many happy, loving people, you are happy and loving. If you constantly see pain and judgment, you are in pain and judgmental. This is what you see in others, whether or not you see it in yourself. What you say to others is a reflection of what you see in yourself. You see yourself in others and you communicate what you see in yourself. Confusing isn't it? It's like a puzzle where everything is backwards. Like Alice in Wonderland, you are in the room of mirrors. Everything is inside out and backward.

You can't really see yourself when you look internally. Think about it. How could you? When you think about yourself, you're not being yourself. Who's doing the thinking if you're thinking about yourself? What are you looking at if you're looking at you? You are the looker, not the thing you're looking at. It's like a cat chasing its tail. There is no way to win at this game.

If you believe what others tell you about yourself you'll be equally confused. Others cannot see you either. A person who truly is non-judgmental and honest will not tell you about you. This person will see you as a non-judgmental and honest person who is constantly changing and being in the light. There is no reason to chastise you if the person is in the light. This person sees everyone as being in the light and being appropriately where he/she is. This person also knows that any judgment or negativity that he/she sees in another is a reflection of his/her own inadequacies. This person will then self-heal, and there is no reason to reveal what was seen. A person who is enlightened—in the light—will not criticize or judge you. The person will not tell you how to change or what to be. The definition and vibration of what and who they are will not allow that.

So what happens when someone criticizes you? You get to see what that person thinks about himself/herself. You get insight into his/her self-character, not yours.

The spirit of the being known as Buddha

Fun; Neutrality; Acceptance

L et's talk about fun. You want to enjoy life but maybe you feel unworthy. You see yourself as ornery, serious, or critical; or you pick some other frailty which you feel makes you unworthy of happiness. Terrible and more terrible. You're being a human again, aren't you? You forgot. It's human nature to have certain "frailties" that are expressed at times. Humans get to experience all the emotions, not just some of the emotions. It's important to integrate all of the parts of the human experience. So, you're going to get them—the jealousies, the anger and occasional hatred. But, it isn't you, is it? You, as a spirit, do not get angry, jealous or critical, do you?

Neutrality. Neutrality. I love that word. I love that concept. It is a balance of all forces and leads to a balance of all emotions, thoughts, and bodily functions. Neutrality in motion is the optimal situation to be in. Are you having fun when you're neutral? Try to experience a state of neutrality now. Remove yourself from the negative and positive thoughts and beliefs for a moment, if you can. Now, from this place, what do you feel like doing?

Now look at this one step further. Are you having fun when you're angry? Do you enjoy yelling at people, or being hurt by others? Perhaps you say, "No," but realize that occasionally it's fun to yell. You release the anger that's pent up inside of you.

So you have fun when you experience negative emotions, as well as positive emotions. Don't fret. You are not alone now. Why do you think comics are so important in the world? They often speak about uncomfortable or anger-producing experiences. They are sarcastic and express negativity, and people laugh at them. Fun is not in the experience itself, but in the enjoyment of the experience. You can have fun in a blistering rainstorm. You can have fun in a sticky or bad situation. How is that? It is because you are enjoying this objective space of neutrality and acceptance.

So you have your answer. How do you have fun? Become neutral and accepting. Be in that space and you will have fun. No matter what you do, you'll enjoy it. And, you'll find that you do not do things that you do not enjoy when you are being in a place of neutrality. You will find that you naturally gravitate toward occupations that interest you. You will remain in a state of observation and will find that you will gravitate toward situations where you want to observe something. Television is an excellent example of this. You can remain neutral, flick through numerous channels, and just watch. Life will fly before you and you are not attached to any of it. This can be fun.

Now pause for a moment and just sit with this information. What do you want to do? You're in a place of just being, of acceptance—a space of no plans and no expectations. You have nothing pulling at you and nothing disagreeing with you.

You are open and light when in a space of neutrality. Can you be hurt by criticism now? No. You're allowing it. You're completely open to being made fun of, so there's no room for anyone to make fun of you. You've filled up the space. Can you now help others to have fun with you? No, no, no, no and no. You can't help others to do anything for themselves. People have to have their own fun.

You notice that some people are more fun to be with. What is it that others like to be around? They like smiles, laughter, lightness of spirit, silliness, acceptance of life, acceptance of themselves, and relaxed charm from allowing life to unfold and not trying to create it. People like to be around others who are having fun. And how do you have fun? Stay in neutral and be amused.

There isn't much to complain about when we're laughing, is there? We just can't think of anything serious to talk about. Are we missing the truth? If churches and temples were places where people came to laugh, would the truth be missed? Or, would it flow from the hearts through the laughter.

I'm speaking, of course, of loving laughter—not sarcasm or biting humor, but light-hearted, in-love-with-life humor. It is impossible to be out of the light of God when laughing in love. In fact, it's impossible not to feel love when laughing. Try it. Not negative humor, though, but positive fun and funnies. When you can laugh, if you can even smile, you are closer to God.

The spirit of the being known as Metatron

The Value of Change

Greetings. I am Metatron. Do you remember my last writing? We were speaking of ancestral hierarchies and the pursuance of joy in one's life. Now I'd like to take this step a little further. Are you familiar with the Thames River, in London, England?

It was not always called this, but it has always been that river. Do you see what I'm talking about? Times change; people change and move to new places. They identify themselves and their surroundings by their knowledge and information at the time—and so the river becomes a newly named river. Now it is looked upon differently as a means of commerce and not merely a barrier to the other side or a means of bathing. It is true of humans, as well. Humans are not always in the same place or at the same time in their lives, yet they tend to expect themselves to be viewed upon as they were several years and even decades ago.

The world has changed drastically since you were born. You look at movies of the 1950s and see older model cars and black

& white television sets. There was no way to transport sound other than through the radio. Phones, stereos, and other means of communication were all stationary. Nowadays you travel everywhere with sound—you even cook with it. You are in a new world, and though you are essentially the same, you are seen differently and have different things to offer.

As people grow, it is important that they continually reevaluate their position in life, making certain it is where they want to be. For instance, your job or career may have been a wonderful choice years ago, but now you are not the same. New opportunities await you. Your available resources have grown. It is time to write the story of how people can change themselves and their lives.

For instance, if a person is not satisfied, how can he or she learn to love and be happy in life? If a person is straining to compose a sonnet when he or she is no longer interested in music, the product will be inferior. It is not possible to move fluidly in life and grow as the soul intended if you stay locked into the same position, beliefs, and subterfuges of life. It is not beneficial to analyze why you want something, then steal it because you do not see another way of getting it. It is not beneficial to harm someone and then justify the action in good faith. You can answer all sorts of calls and beliefs within you, but you cannot alter or direct your energies productively if you are not first helping yourself to change with the times.

Remember that there is a time for everything. When it is time to change, the past habits will only bring you pain and suffering. If you are lost and want to find a new home, looking in the old neighborhoods won't be productive. Change is essential.

Change is important. Change is what life is. We are not mere stones that grow throughout millenniums. We are of human origin and are taking the time to heal and grow with the times.

What is done during this transition is not important, but it IS important that the transition to a new life be allowed to occur. Fighting change will not benefit you. Resisting new opportunities will not benefit you, either. It is time to change—and change you will. You can be dragged kicking and screaming, or you can walk or leap. The choice is yours.

When you follow your soul's journey, you find you are energized and strengthened. You will be happy and alert. If you drag your feet and resist what you know in your heart you must do, you will fail. Do not look around you at how others are living their lives. This is not relevant to you. Do not ask for favors of others to help you be entertained. You are self-entertaining when you are on your own course. You must find that course and then follow it without evaluating how others look, what they think, how it compares, and if it is productive.

You must not ask, "Why am I doing this?" Sometimes there is an answer, but often there is no answer. Life isn't made to be planned and scoped out. It is made to be lived and enjoyed.

Yes, you see others who have planned and dictated their lives so that they are now in profitable positions and in the exact place they expected to be. That is rare. When you look at these people, you'll see that they have not changed at all. So it is easy for them to continue on with the same life. Some people do this in good faith. Some do it by lying to themselves. Most people change throughout their lives, but do not honor the change— and they suffer.

Time for honoring of the soul is essential to everyone's growth. Time for living and loving in spirit is so important, and yet so ignored. Many are walking around as if they are just automatons on conveyor belts. So many people react to the environment instead of creating their reality. So many are unhappy because they do not honor the strivings and desires of the heart. They are tied to obligations, habits, and remorse.

Many people are now wondering about what they want to do with their lives. I look around and they are searching, but there is no goal in sight. They fret because they are ready for change, but they don't know where to go.

These people are searching for guidance from their soul, but are looking outside of themselves. They are saddened because this guidance is not forthcoming. This is the case because there is no direction but to the soul. In order to find one's purpose and love, one must look to the soul. This is not found in books, on the radio, or in self-help classes. It is only found by going within and following. Sometimes it's not helpful to immediately quit what you are doing just because there is no clear path. But when a sign occurs, it is important to follow it. When life changes and tells you to move or change, go with this. Settling for status quo when newness and dreams begin to unfold is disappointing to you as well as those around you.

It is remarkable how we all just float through life. Then an opportunity knocks that seems so far from the present reality, yet is somehow exciting and different. There's a calling that is unsettling. This call is from the heart.

The spirit of the being known as Elanora

Emotions and Intellect

Hello. I am Elanora, an angel, and I'd like to speak to you about the role of the female on Earth. When we relate from our female nature, there is much less that needs to be said.

This is the dilemma of the female. The feminine energy is essential to the functioning of all that is. It is an important aspect and so necessary. Yet it is not intellectual in the usual sense. The feminine is knowing, self-containing, and all-encompassing of the inner beauty. But words are somewhat foreign when in this state. The language seems more feminine, more poetic, less rational, and somehow less believable if you're listening or reading with the male side of yourself. The conversation between us, as women, will be more free-flowing. The energy will move more quickly, and the emotions will fly by and alight, then take off again. It gets very frantic and giggly, then stops. And we sit staring in each other's eyes and just being.

We want to sit and hang out. We understand each other, although we can't explain why. The male side screams out, "What does it mean? What are you saying? How can I fit it into some sort of box-like structure and pin your words down?" It can't. The feminine can't be tied down or rationalized from the voice of the intellect. It is not intellectually based. The feminine is heart based. The feminine is inwardly knowing and resides in the heart of the soul.

I'm not saying that the male is not of true heart any more than I'm saying that the feminine can't speak, think, or be intellectual. It is just that the center of the attention (the center of balance) is in another spot. Women love to emote. They are closer to the emotions. Men—or the male sides of everyone—want answers to questions and need to know the logical meaning so they can plan and do, and plan and create, and do and do more.

Women can just BE. The female experiences the world as a whole, not a continuum. She sees everything through her heart, and so there is no concept of time when someone is being completely and entirely female. Time and anything linear becomes irrelevant, almost nonsensical. Women can talk for hours and lose track of time. (From now on let me clarify that when I say "woman" or "man" I am referring to the energy and not the form. Everyone has both sides. Most are more oriented to one side or the other.)

It is difficult to stay in one place in one's thoughts when being female. Female attention wavers and flits like a humming-bird. Then she can come right back to where she was without skipping a beat in a conversation or a task. How many things do you have going on at once? Yes, it's called multi-tasking, and women are masters of it. It is essential when raising a child. It's important to realize that the many focuses of your energy are not inappropriate when you're being feminine. It's expected.

So you ask why we aren't seeing more dialogues with Masters who are women. It is because the women let the men do the talking. Women listen. They heal and they nurture. Women are just being and growing in that being-ness. Women are the heart and core, not the part that communicates and roars.

Every man you have spoken with was and is supported by women. Every angel has both aspects of its character, which it values and cherishes. It is not possible to reach high levels of enlightenment without honoring both the male and female in oneself. It is essential in the understanding of all creation that you review and view life through both sides of yourself. But when you come to center and want to just know the God Source, you will know it from the place of stillness. It is from the place of oneness that we know what it is to just BE.

Many women on the planet struggle with this mere being-ness. It is not seen as a worthy endeavor. Women are not honored when they merely exist and support. Everyone on this planet now seems to judge themselves by what they do, not who they are. Well, of course not everyone, but so many humans. It is important to be productive and creative; but what of creating from the heart? What of creating from a knowing of what is important to the soul? How is that not honored?

The intellect will plan and scheme and the ego is elated when the ends justify the process. But what about merely knowing what is needed and expressing this to the Creator from the heart? Then the event just happens in a way that is provided by the Creator. It is unique and totally fulfilling.

Women are emotional in many ways. There are far too few definitions of emotions. They are bagged together into lumps, such as the "anger" lump, the "sad" lump, and so forth. There are many forms of anger. You are angry toward your spouse in a way that is different from when you are angry with the store clerk. You say it is the same, but notice that it's different. You say there is one type of love—and in truth, everything is love in action—but there are many types of love: love of a man and woman, love of a child, love of an aunt, love of an in-law, and so forth. What I'm trying to say here is that there are so many forms of emotions including love, anger, and grief. You can't categorize them. You can merely say, "I'm being more involved in my emotional self now." This is because your emotions will mirror the situation and the climate. The emotions are like a stream—fluid and ever changing.

Imagine sitting by a brook and you can hear it talking to you. It makes sounds like conversation and as the water rushes over the rocks in different ways, and with different force and temperature, it made different sounds. They are musical and almost conversational. That is a perfect description of the emotions.

Now that is not something the intellect respects. The intellect sees this energy as frivolous and pointless and meaningless…I could go on and on. It is not important what the intellect says about the emotions. The intellect is just one aspect of self, just as the emotions are. However, without all of the aspects, a human would be faltering and ineffectual.

The emotions tune you into the finer aspects of the vibration of life. The emotions are like a tuning fork that is mirroring to you what is going on inside yourself and in your environment. The emotions talk to you and say, "I am joyous. I am sad. I am unhappy. I am frivolous and therefore sad. I was angry, but not anymore...." You see, they are constantly moving and are a perfect barometer of what is going on with a person on Earth.

It is very important to honor these emotions. I'm not saying to run your life by them, anymore than you'd want to run your life by the intellect alone. The emotions need to be integrated into the whole. They need to be honored, allowed, and nurtured; then they will rescue you from boredom, pull you into glorious situations of light and joy, and keep you out of harm. The emotions will mirror another aspect of what is important to you.

If you are unhappy, you need to move in another direction. Honor this. If you are angry, you are being taken advantage of. Honor this. You are expressing a part of yourself that is experiencing life as you know it. If you are not honoring it, you are not clearly on your path and are not in heart.

Get carried away sometimes by the emotions. Let them show you another aspect of life. Honor and enjoy them. Whether they are pleasant or sour, they are a part of you—a necessary part of you.

The spirit of the being known as Lao Tsu

The Quiet Mind

How do you still your continuous thoughts? It seems that when you are meditating you become distracted with visions, concerns, thoughts, and plans about your day. These are often productive thoughts. Your mind is actively working on tasks that it cannot often approach during the day when you are busy. You are actively pursuing many things, and the mind is busy most of the time on the tasks at hand.

It is thought that the only purpose of meditation is to still the mind to reach the higher parts of the soul. This is an appropriate action for meditation. It is very worthwhile to do this. There is also a time to meditate to reach the Higher Mind. Your mind has many aspects, including reaching your Higher Self and giving you information it can use in form. For instance, you may have ideas to call someone, or to tell someone something important. These insights are not noticed when you're answering phones, typing, or working in whatever form—and certainly not when you're talking with others. It's difficult to hear the Higher Mind when you're busy.

So you find that when you meditate, your mind begins to interrupt your reverie to show you visions and tell you things about your future, past, and present. It seems distracting; but it is like a child pulling at its mother's skirt, saying, "I need some attention. I have something to say." And you're saying, "Not now, dear. Go away. I'm busy." Then you do not give it another opportunity to rejoice with you.

Let your mind wander sometimes and you will find that if you follow it closely, it will give you clues into itself and its higher workings. It's important to give yourself some creative thinking time. Let your mind wander and spout its peace. Let it tell you what it has found, what it longs for, what it knows, and what it fears. It is important to know your own mind thusly, uninterrupted and unencumbered by others and other parts of the self.

Your mind is a valuable tool and aspect of yourself. You honor it with intelligence tests and other displays of activity, but you do not often realize its full potential. The mind is as expansive as any other aspect of the Universe. It can reach into other realms and bring you information and ideas. It can be a creative force in your life, if you let it.

Some believe that the goal of meditation and proper living is to merely still the mind. This is only one small beginning aspect of the meditation process. It is then important to watch the mind and allow it to have free reign to go where it will, with some guidance. You do not want to dwell on painful or unsavory images. One or two glances will do. Then let it express itself.

If you write down your thoughts, you'll be surprised to realize how often your mind gives you the same information and how often it is not heeded. The mind is a valuable tool and an important aspect of your inheritance as a human being. Use it. Allow it to think. Let it fly and then honor and listen to it.

You have a "child" nagging at your feet. What do you do? Stop for a moment and listen to it. Honor it and write down what it tells you. Or, at best, tell it you'll speak to it later. Then make time for it. Allow yourself time to think. Let your thoughts go and honor them. Write them down. Give yourself a mind break—not a break FROM the mind but a break FOR the mind. Let it speak to you. Get to know it. It can be your best friend and a worthy employee.

There is a concern that if you give the mind time to think, you will then be plagued by constant interruptions. Do not see these thoughts as interruptions. See them as the adversarial workings of your employee, sitting at the next desk. He's on the phone, or talking, or thinking out loud; but you don't have to listen to him. You can go on about your business. You don't have to shut him up. Would you lean over and ask your employee at work to shut up and stop being what he is or stop doing what he's doing because you're busy? No, you know that your employee is doing his job and you let him.

It is the same with the mind. It will run continuously. It is the nature of the beast, so to speak. I will change that phrase because it is not actually beast-like. It is the nature of that part of the animal. It thinks. That's what minds do. However, where you put your attention IS your business. If you have a difficult time not paying attention to the mind's constant thinking, then you have another problem to consider.

You do not need to change the mind. You need to find a way to filter your attention so that you can pay attention to only what you need to hear at the time. If you honor this and give the time to think with your full attention, you find that you are less distracted by it. You will know it well and will honor it more. Then you can make a conscious decision to not listen to it because you will know when it's telling you something important and when it's wandering aimlessly. You are the master of your own mind. You are not its slave. You can listen when you want, use it when you desire, and ignore it completely if you choose. Believe me, some people do ignore it, unfortunately. I'm sure you know someone like this. "You're not thinking," means that the person is not paying attention to what is being thought. The mind is always at work.

For example, perhaps you're involved in a task and you are interrupted by a thought that does not relate to the task at hand. The mind says, "Call your friend who had surgery," or some such information. You take note of this thought and continue on with your task. You then call your friend soon thereafter. Or, you interrupt your task and call immediately. Your mind did you a service, and now you are back to attending to your task. Did you get hurt or inconvenienced in the process? No, you were helped to remember something. This is a good example of appropriate mind control. You totally immersed yourself in the thought you were having, made a note of it, and brought yourself back to the task at hand.

This is the beauty of the mind, and the heart, and all of the aspects of your humanness. You have all parts working at the same time. You can honor them and pay attention to each one in its time. The emotions, the mind, and the body all have much to offer you.

The spirit of the being known as Metatron

Finding Fulfillment

You may or may not live a full life, but there are most likely times when you feel unfulfilled. When you say you are unfulfilled, what part of you is speaking? Is your body feeling healthy? Is it cleansed, exercised, and even healed? Is your mind satisfied? Are you being creative and learning more about yourself and others? Are you having fun with your hobbies and being charitable? Are you communicating with friends and family? What is missing?

You'll find that you are happiest when you feel the oneness—your connection to the Source. That is what everyone is seeking now. People are quitting their jobs, leaving their relationships, changing residences, and trying all sorts of antics to find the missing ingredient in their lives. It is not love that they seek. It is the connection with God that they lack when feeling unfulfilled.

How do you go about experiencing this connection? Go to the Source. Know that you are seeking God and your connection to the God Source. Even the act of seeking will help you to feel less depressed and more satisfied. If you know that your main function on this planet is to bring heaven to Earth, then all you have to do is know God and be where and how you are. When you know God, you can watch television with God; you can go for a walk with God; you can make love with a partner and both of you will bring God to life. Do you feel God now?

What is your purpose? It is the same as that of anyone here. You are trying to bring the energy of the God Source through you and bring it to life. If you're not doing that, you're doing the wrong thing and won't be fulfilled. If you're not happy where you are, connect more fully with God and you will know what to do next and where to go.

Listen to me now. What does the heart say to you more than anything else? Do more of whatever your heart longs to do and you will be happier. Do more of what fulfills you. Be in that state of fulfillment and when you leave it, get back to it.

Even in your work or job there is a task that is fulfilling; a way of doing something that is rewarding; a way of relating to it that is inspiring. In every job there is a door to God, but if you have too much difficulty finding it, seek another job. Do not stay in a place that is unfulfilling.

Do not feel that you are unable or unqualified for another form of work or job. Do what you love. For example, if you love working on cars, keep your job and do the car work on the side. Eventually you'll be so good at auto work that you'll have a job at it. If there is nothing you love, get in touch with yourself through meditation or yoga (or through some other form or practice) with the express purpose of finding who you are and what you love. Seek out the God of your heart and you will find your own fulfillment.

Even everyday tasks and activities that seem unproductive are appropriate if they fulfill you. Of course they have to be healthy and inspiring (and legal), as well. If you are doing only what you think you should be doing because you feel you must, you will not be fulfilled. I'm not telling you to release your obligations. I'm telling you to move within the structure of the life you've created and then let your heart guide you.

If you have a child and feel unfulfilled, you are remiss. Find the joy in your heart for the child and follow your heart. If you have a job, find the joy in your heart and find what you're supposed to be doing there. You cannot leave your child, but you can find a new way for the two of you to experience life together. If you cannot leave your job, you can find a way to move into an area that you love more and eventually be where you need to be within your life.

I know of a woman who was a belt maker in a factory. She sewed belts every day. She was not unhappy, though, because she was thinking about candies as she sewed. She was creating candies in her head. Soon she began to experiment with making them. She tried them out on her friends. Some were well accepted and some weren't. She altered her recipes and tried again. Eventually she was a success at candy making and began selling her candies at work. She looked forward to work because her monotonous job gave her the opportunity to sell more candies and make up more recipes. Eventually she had so many orders that she had to quit her job. She now owns a very successful candy shop and she loves sharing her creations with her customers.

I can name you several stories about those who followed their hearts and did what they loved. It is not difficult. However, just thinking about it will not get you there. Do what you love or find a way to love what you do. That is the only key to success and fulfillment. And, when you are doing what you love, you will be bringing heaven to Earth and you will be enlightened and happy.

The spirit of the being known as Metatron

Creating a New World; 9/11

Ten days have passed since the disaster of 9/11. There is much sadness and processing that we are doing, as well. This is not an easy time at any level. The future of the human race is unclear now. Certainly we see difficult times ahead. Your government is forging ahead like a headstrong bull, ready to plow down anything in its path. It moves like a force field ready to show its strength. There is a light burning in the people. This fuel is not reflected in the government at this time. There is much anger and angst. It is unpleasant to watch. There is great concern here for the lives of many.

Be not so easy to judge. Realize that the events that have transpired have catapulted you into a new awareness and level of compatibility. There is much love growing between all of you because of this tragedy. I am not justifying the acts of the terrorists. Still, look to the light and see the beauty of the events as they unfold. Build on this love. Mourn, as we mourn here, and remember that we will all heal from this tragedy. Then thank God for the grace that is still present and building between us.

Your planet is actually shaking from the reverberations of this event. There is an actual vibration that is still occurring on the Earth from the emotions and physical events that occurred. It affects you all, though you are not aware of it. Actually, all of you are experiencing the feelings and emotions of all of those around you, in your towns and throughout the world. You are more aware of these feelings and emotions on a subconscious level.

Some of those of you who are clairaudient heard voices from New York—the voices of rescue workers—sentences flying at you from out of the ethers and into your head, as if these people were standing next to you. You may have heard, "Move back. An ambulance needs to get by," and similar phrases—people talking among themselves. This occurred because the grid shifted and the magnetics of the planet are altered and rearranging themselves. The planetary magnetism is shifting and the energies that were present before are rapidly deteriorating. You are rebuilding with a new force field. We are assisting you. It is tenuous work, as it cannot be planned. It must be built moment by moment as we move toward the light.

It is so important that there is no anger or hostility at this time, as it will be built into the new field. Remember that we are creating a New World.

There is great love and appreciation of you, and your offers and attempts to heal others and to assist in the Universal efforts that are taking place. It is this love and light that heals the angels and Masters. Our salvation, and the salvation of all, lies in your love and the love of those in body at this time. You are the hope we seek.

It is important to have faith in yourself at this time. Be yourself. Know you are enough. Stand tall and know that no matter the outcome, you will survive and move on. The light of God never dies. Be not in fear, as you will always be with God. Hold on to nothing now. Recreate a new life as you go. Build a future, and you will be able to handle whatever transpires. You are light warriors and you are awakening the light warriors in each other.

Many are now banding together to reform new soul groups and bonds. It is a great union that is occurring. No matter the outcome, you will retain this growth and light. Remember this. Use these times to be strong and loving. Release your selfishness and love yourself. Release your fears and love everyone you meet. Stand tall now in the face of adversity and you will win the war, no matter the outcome of the battle.

Say that you love God and mean it. That is your true salvation. For the light of the Lord is in us all, and the love of God is a love that is never broken. God lives. Your love lives. You live forever in the face of the Lord.

It is a lot to ask you as a human to let go of your attachment to form. You may lose your body at this time, but you will never lose your heart and soul when you are bonded in spirit with the One. I am not predicting your death. I am merely suggesting that you do not fear it. Your fear will lead you to darkness. Know that you are always protected in spirit in the light of the Lord.

Listen to your body. Love it. It is a precious gift. It is an honor to be present on Earth at this time. There are great emotions, terrible burdens, and wonderful opportunities for growth. You are now able to fully experience the full range of emotions on the planet, and you can choose the light with full wisdom of the darkness. It is not easy to see what an opportunity this is while in body. Trust that you are blessed. Always know that we are here with you.

The spirit of the beings known as Metatron and Michael

The Great Energy Shift

Metatron: There has been a shift in the level of consciousness since 9/11, yet there is still little change in the way many are doing business. I know you may see yourself acting differently, but for the most part, do you see that others are acting the same? They go about the same business and have the same goals. There is much talk about global peace and growth in consciousness, and there is a banding together of others who were not previously connected. How is it that there is not change in the daily routine to match the level of consciousness that you say is occurring?

It's troubling to me. I feel that a call to action must be made to honor this shift, where all people make just one small alteration in their lives; just one small shift to show each other that there is a door that has opened for a new way to exist on the planet; just one ray of hope from each person that life as we know it is changing and growing.

I honor all on the planet and do not criticize those who are in body. I would like those of you who have bodies to realize the great shift that has taken place in the general consciousness and to embody it. I'm seeing that it is not being acknowledged. Do you understand this?

You can shift or change anything, really: a change in what is normally eaten for breakfast to one that is healthier; a new resolve and follow-through to exercise more; a way to take time off each day to meditate, even in the middle of the day; any action to honor the transitional times that are occurring.

Michael: It is remarkable how the people on the planet are banding together in war, but are not full of hate, as they have been in the past. I especially am grateful that there is no killing in the streets and no animosities between you. I know there are some isolated incidents of prejudice, but this is small compared to what it could be. Honor this in yourselves. See how far you've come in peacetime.

The tone of the energy has shifted, as well. There is less of a hum of disregard and more of an honoring of the abilities, talents, and strengths of each of you. You are all more tolerant of each other. This new tolerance is powerful enough to shift the level of your energy a thousand-fold. The repercussions of this type of shift will be remarkable.

Metatron: I am noticing great strife in other areas of the world, and there is fear that the United States will crumble and the world will fall to tyranny. The U.S. has been thought of as a giant among people of other countries. The U.S. offers freedom to the world. Other countries have history and culture, but the United States embodies the concept of life as a free person.

It is very troublesome for those in other countries to see the U.S. attacked and faltering. They are horrified by this attack, as if it threatens them personally. The entire world is looking both spiritually and physically at the citizens of the United States to see how well they respond. Those in the U.S. are all models for others to follow in times of strife.

Even in these crucial times there is always room for laughter. It is not a sacrilege to enjoy life, even when there is suffering and death around. Honor the beauty of the times and find joy in being able to be on the planet at this remarkable time. Each and every one of you is so strong in your ability to remain in these troubled and pressured times. Rejoice in that and laugh. It will heal the heart.

The spirit of the being known as Metatron

Honoring Life

There is much to be done now, and there is also much time to do it in. It is illusional that you see a time line and a definitive period of change. Change is occurring on many levels of consciousness and you cannot alter this energy too quickly or there will be repercussions on other levels.

Take time to rest more. Enjoy yourself and your life. This increases your awareness, as well. Do you notice how emotional you become when you don't rest or find entertainment, even if it seems mindless? Your body needs to rest when your emotions are in turmoil.

You are all so strong in your resolve and adapt to the times quickly. Notice that as the mind adjusts and forges new paths, the emotions and body are slower to follow. It is true that this is an important time, yet there has been a great deal done already. There have been mass movements for global change. Great strides have been taken, and still it is only a few weeks since the time of the incident at the World Trade Center. Listen to your heart and body. Rest more. Take more time for yourself during times of stress. This will allow you the privilege of giving more to others and contemplating great change meditationally.

Take note of your accomplishments every day. I notice that there is a great movement to plan out each day; to look at the next day and follow through with the goals and appointments set forth. It would also not be extravagant to look at the accomplishments of the previous day, as well. Take time to push yourself forward, and also take time to honor and reward yourself.

Look at even the little things that you do during the day. Connect with those you see only briefly, such as looking into the eyes of the bank teller or the grocery checkout clerk, and honoring her. This little gesture can help her, if only for a moment. These little moments and incidents on your part add up. They make a difference. Honor them, whether it be a kind word on the phone to a friend, or a large donation to a charity. It all makes a difference in the light of the Universe.

Another aspect that I see concerns the taking of charity to a new level. There is great giving with little thought to receiving going on. In the past there have been great affairs to honor charities, where the givers also benefited. Now there are many people just donating for no apparent reason other than to give and help. This is remarkable; it is quite a shift. Notice how likely it is that this will continue. A new level of giving has begun both on the individual level as well globally.

It is time for all to honor the beauty of the planet. Let each of you appreciate the extraordinariness of nature. Each petal of a flower is an art form. Honor your surroundings. I'm not preaching political upheaval in an environmental sense; although it is important to give love back to the Almighty through appreciation of all that is provided—especially when you are in a body. It is an honor to be here on Earth at this time. Simply put, there is a great magnificence in being a part of the intricacies of God and life in this way. You are experiencing the utmost in refinement of the God Source. Honor it and rejoice in it. Do not attempt to redo it or to alter it in a great way. Know that the Lord has provided for you in great measure, so respond accordingly.

Listen to your voice when it says to harm nothing around you. Honor each aspect of the creation, and in turn it will honor you. Be not a destroyer, but a creator on the planet. Then you will reap the rewards of all its bounty and abundance. Honor even the little aspects, such as a spring shower or a falling golden leaf. The chirping of the crickets at night and the glowing of the moon through the trees are both miraculous wonders. Being able to taste, feel, and experience love in a physical form are all wonders that you need to acknowledge and not take for granted.

It is gratifying for us to watch as you delight in absorbing the sun's rays. Rejoice in the sunlight. Feel the energy of the moon as she rises. Know the beauty of a waterfall and the peace of sitting by a stream or by the ocean. Know these things in your daily life and rejoice in them. Smell the flowers and honor them. Sense the other animals around you and pay attention to them, as they do to you. You have countless opportunities to interact with animals of many different types. Is this not remarkable? Yet most of you walk by the birds, squirrels, and even other humans without any acknowledgement.

It is a difficult time, in truth; yet each moment is remarkable. View the overall beauty and perfection around you; and the events of the world, even those as traumatic and devastating as those of late, will pale in comparison. Your hearts hurt from the loss of your brothers and sisters who were a part of the incidents on September 11. You still are great warriors on the planet, surrounded by natural beauty and abundance, animals, and other people. Rejoice in this, as well.

The spirit of the being known as Shakti

The Power of Emotions

The female spirit is one and the same in all women on the planet and in the ethers. It is easy to come into body in either form because the body is a dense projection of the spirit, and we all have both male and female energy in our aura and in our essential natures. Yet in spirit we embody one aspect more predominantly. In this discussion I would like to address those who are more female by nature.

In many ways people have underestimated the power of the female, thereby seeing a strong and directed nature as being male. In truth, it is the power of the female that governs and drives you. Many women have learned to channel this feminine energy through the face of manly power. You use your mind to project your female power, as this is more male in nature. This is a learned response governed by the needs of your time and place. If women were in power you would not be doing this. When the woman is able to show herself in her true power, the Earth will reign as a complete entity. For now we are in the midst of a severe and powerful shift in the energies of mankind.

The female energy leads us into deep meditation and astral travel. This is a feminine trait. As women we want to go inward and experience the delights of our deeply feminine gardens. We are inwardly as full and rich as the world is outwardly detailed and extraordinary.

Can you imagine having an entire world inside of you? This is not a euphemism. This is a reality. You could spend as much time exploring the inward nature as you do the outward manifestations of life. There is much credence given to the outward manifestations because the world is now male oriented. In past times, there was much less pursuing of worldly goods, with more direction and central focus on the inward pursuits. We were all grounded in our essential natures and there was a lot less relating on the earthly plane with direct and verbal communications.

Telepathy was prominent. Feelings were worn on our bodies as indicators of our true aspect at the time. It was not unusual to cry when walking about, nor was it unusual to laugh for no apparent reason. Emotions were not fly-by-night, but were outward manifestations of our true awareness on a deeper level.

Let me see if I can clarify this difference. In the world you live in now emotions are seen as trivial and base. It is felt that they are nuisances that must be dealt with and acknowledged. The emotions are not seen as being directly relevant to reality, but as some inert manifestation of an unproductive aspect of oneself.

This was not always true. In times past, humans were more feminine in nature and the outward manifestations of emotions were honored as the mirrors to the soul. The projections of the soul's journey are often portrayed through the emotions. Let's say you are feeling anxious and nervous when you are near a certain individual. You think you must control these feelings, move forward in sincerity and strength, and continue to be with this person. In times past, we would have not moved forward, but would have honored the nervousness and anxiety as indications that we were not ready to pursue this line of communication and intertwining of energy.

It is true that we are often mislead by our emotions in this way. We are anxious because of fear, and are lead to be stagnant because we do not want to experience new horizons. These are not the fears I am referring to. Such references will be clearer as you learn to honor the emotions more. It will become more natural to experience the emotions. Therefore, you will be able to differentiate between emotions based upon the fear of change and those based upon the fear of not being able to deal with another's energy.

This is simple, really. If you are nervous being around another person, step back. Honor your emotions and go inward to your Source to check out your knowledge of the situation. You will note that this feeling is driving you to search your internal "data base." There may be new information that you need before you move forward with this person. There may be a need for more inward strength.

You can tap into your knowledge base—your internal wisdom—and feed off of this information. Then as you move forward, this new information will lead you to know whether you are in fear because of doubt or not wanting to move in the wrong direction. Take heed of your emotions and honor them. They are true indicators of the wisdom and communications of your soul.

Emotions are not like thoughts. They do not directly inform you of specific reasons why something must or must not be done. They do not work in this way. Instead, rely on your emotions to prompt you into thought. Let your analyzer work for you, whether you are in fear or in happiness. Tune into it and see what information is being pulled up or made available when you are sensing something emotionally.

It is important to honor all aspects of yourself and to find the time to respect them. For these aspects of self are true indicators—beacons of the real truth underlying the workings of the soul interactions between you and others. Always honor your emotions as the key to your soul force. They are a barometer of how you are in your life, and where you want to be in your heart of hearts.

The New Millenium

Simpler times are on the way for many of the warriors of this generational schema. The path is set and the obstacles are slowly moving. The result will be a change in the modus operandi of the planetary system. The people of the Earth will no longer be privy to all of the privileges without guidance. The awareness of the individuals on the planet will shift to include the realization and understanding of the spiritual guides. Looked to as the elders of the planet, such as the tribal chiefs or ancient healers of old, these spirits will guide those who are in need. They will also clear the path and have more influence over the outcome of possible negative events. It will no longer be possible to wreak such havoc on others—to harm each other to such an extent. Those who continue to do so will eventually be eliminated from the genetic pool.

A new generation is beginning and they will form the beginnings of the new millennial shift. The outcome will be a planetary system that will move to include the higher levels of consciousness and the lower levels of experiential knowledge. Both sides of the astral will benefit from this. It will be possible for humans on the earth plane to learn from the experiences of the other life forms. It will also be possible for spiritual beings to inhabit the experiential levels (not the bodies) of the humans on Earth. To a great extent these spiritual beings can share in and influence the experiences and judgments of the people.

This was not and is not possible at this time. As it stands, all of us are attuned to the humans on the planet, but cannot interfere or disrupt the processes these humans are going through. It is painful to watch at times, humorous at others. It is felt that the growth of the entire universal system would be better served if the humans were again aware of the information from their ancestors and their guides and makers. This knowledge in itself will be a deterrent for future harm of the species upon itself. Humans will know their place and role, and they will not attempt to alter the fate of others. They will also understand the implications of wrong action and wrong direction. This understanding alone will force people to look at their choices more carefully and their motives implicitly. Responsibility will come to those who deserve it through pureness of heart and action.

This change will occur within the next ten or twenty years. It has been occurring since the turn of the century. Prepara-tions have been taking place since that time. Developments in technological and visualization techniques, as well as increases in comfort and communication were essential for the peace and stability of the race. Once these are in place, mankind will be free to move itself into another dimensional realm. This is the fate of the planet. This was foreseen for several millennia and was the intention of the original makers.

The experiment of humans planning their own destiny and lessons is nearing an end. The destiny and plans of all beings will now incorporate the needs of the universal forces and Supreme Being. The experiment was originated to see how beings would interact and grow without supreme intervention on a direct level.

It has been interesting to watch how the voids in universal love and understanding are filled with hostility and selfishness. The need for security has led many to harm themselves and others. However, some have achieved the understanding that all are secure in the force of the Almighty and that it is time to let their knowledge run free. They will again be kind and faithful to the Almighty. These people have gained incredible strength of will and perseverance through the attainment of this goal. It has been gratifying to see how the genetic material of the Godhead recreates itself in these humans.

Others have not been able to break through the barrier of the soul to reach the body mind. These people are less fortunate, but not less loved or less important. All efforts, struggle, and experience are fed directly to the Supreme Being and are a source of understanding. It is not impossible for the Godhead to recreate itself in this manner. Without knowledge of itself in a mirror-like way, the Godhead is unaware of itself. It is not possible to look inside yourself when you ARE yourself. You must create an image of a part of yourself and look at it first. Then watch what happens. How do the parts interact and what are the characteristics of each?

You can do this as humans, but often do not realize what you are doing. When you daydream, you are creating an image of yourself and watching what happens to it. You problem solve when you do this. When you plan or create, when you imagine or think, you are projecting a part of yourself into a specific type of ethereal form and are then looking at it and working through it.

Thought is a projection that the body places into the atmosphere surrounding itself. This energy, which has been projected, affects the greater whole. The ways and differentiation of how this happens is greatly misunderstood. It is not done to control the environment or others around you. You think in order to see the results of your actions. You think so that you can see a part of yourself working and come to know yourself a little better because of it. You think and then you think some more, and you think it is you who is thinking. This is true. It IS you thinking, but it is also the Godhead thinking. The parts become smaller and smaller, as the energy is dispersed throughout the Universe. All parts are mirrors of parts of the greater whole and are seen as such. Once seen, these parts can be changed.

When you think something "evil" you may become aware of the hostility and destruction it causes in your own life. Evil thoughts are projections of parts of yourself that are undeveloped. These thoughts, when manifested into action, become the basis for the crimes and evil actions of humans upon others. You see how these actions affect others. They will then ricochet and hurt you. You also see how the evil actions of others will often cause their own destruction. Evil thoughts (thoughts that cause harm to others, whether implied or articulated) will harm the individual thinking them. This harm may ricochet immediately, or in another lifetime. The soul will remember and eventually learn to understand the implications of these types of thoughts. When this occurs, the soul will watch the thoughts and the response to them. It is then possible to consciously control your thoughts with the intention of creating positive growth for the human.

This is similar to a child who eats too many cookies. The child will become sick and realize that cookies, in mass quantities, are harmful. The child may choose to continue to eat the cookies and suffer, or choose to stop eating the cookies and feel better in mind and body. This is the choice that the individual soul makes when it sees itself making thought choices. Certain thoughts lead to certain actions and specific reactions. In this way the soul watches how a projection of itself will look in the world. The soul can then choose to change itself and its actions.

As you go, so goes God. That is how God sees itself— through you. You are a part of the Godhead projected onto this planet. It is important that you remember this. Then you can learn to watch yourself more closely, or better put, God will learn to watch itself more closely and thereby learn more from itself. You are an integral part of the whole. Remember this and take responsibility for it. You are untimely in your misbehavior when you look upon yourself as an individual. You think that you are an individual entity existing in time. You are not. You are an individual formation of the greater whole. Remember this. It is not so hard to bear. It is a blessing. You are of great importance to the development of this planet. Take your job seriously and enjoy it.

So we begin a new era in the life of humanity. The era of greater understanding has begun and will continue to grow.

There will be a shift in awareness, counteracted by the shifting of the Life Force of some of the species on this planet. There are some that will disappear. Do not hold on to your past. True, you must not harm other species, but you must let them leave if they so desire. There will be other places and times for these beings.

There is a new era coming, and new species will be developed to interact more freely with the human species. These animals can be of great assistance. Take the ravens, for example. They have learned how to interact with those humans who choose to listen. Deborah recently visited one on its perch. She was invited into its head and saw the surrounding landscape. This was a wonderful experience.

Think about how it would be to enter other animals' heads, or learn from their experiences. There will be species that can share other genetic knowledge with you, and you will be able to listen to them. Let this be. Let the other animals that have no more to offer move on. The whales are an old and developed species. They may harbor new and interesting information for you. The dolphins also have lessons to teach. However, these species may not choose to stay with you long. Listen to them now, lest you lose the opportunity for this knowledge.

It may be difficult for you to watch other species die out and leave the Earth. Know that they are a part of the same being, truly; and know that their spirit will not be destroyed, but will continue to serve the greater whole in other ways. Know also that this form can be recreated and reformed, as well. This is not the case with animals that destroy other species. They are eliminated if they destroy without acknowledgement of the Source. The animals that kill for food are performing a required ritual.

Those who needlessly harm others on the planet will eliminate their purpose and will be recycled into a higher form.

Think back on all of the animals you've known and how they have influenced you. Animals are non-subtle forms of the manifestation of Higher Spirit. They may not talk to you, but they lend energy and amusement to your life. The birds sing for you. The cardinals are beautiful to watch. Whales dance in the water and put on water shows. There are many such instances where life is entertaining because of the animals in it.

Then there are times when animals have rescued humans, at great risk to themselves. Animals will perform actions that may seem strange to humans. Do not undervalue them, however. Look at them, not as lesser beings, but as different beings. Then see what they have to teach you. See how they move and act in life. Communicate with them, if you can. If not, see how they communicate with you. Each part is a mirror of the Almighty.

Do not kill animals unless you need to eat them. Do not eat them unless you absolutely need this form of food. Your body knows what's best and necessary. Your tongue is often ruled by the emotional body and not the physical. It is essential that you learn to listen to your body and its needs, and then follow this. Otherwise you will be impeding your growth. You can look at yourself and notice how your emotions control your mind and tongue. But how long will you watch? Change it. Enough.

You need a strong, flexible, and awake body to function as a guide and mirror unto yourself. Take care of the body and it will serve you well. Take advantage of it and you will lose your opportunity to grow and change.

As humans, you have inhabited this planet for thousands of

years. It is unfortunate that we have not had the opportunity to grow more. Still, a lot has been done. It has been an interesting experiment—one that will forever feed the annals of the history of the species. Your efforts and actions have been a source of knowledge and inspiration to many species in many planes of existence. Now we all look forward to the growth as the planet moves into this new era. A new millennium is upon us. A celebration and congratulations of enormous proportion will echo throughout the Universe. Enjoy this. You have served us all well and we welcome you into the force of the knowing.

The Writings of the Masters

Part Two

Unedited Dialogues With The Masters & Angels

The spirit of the being known as Buddha

Remembering Who You Are

Buddha: *Today is the day you remember who you are.*

Deborah: And who are you?

Buddha: *I am the one you call the Buddha. It is my energy you feel. Do you not know me by now?*

Deborah: I do somewhat, but like to be certain.

Buddha: *Ah, tempting to value the ego so much that you have to doubt your own intuition and knowing. You are better than that. You are an intelligent and sensitive being. There are not many like you. That is why you don't fit in quite like others. That does not mean you are a misfit. It means you are different; delightful and different.*

It is common for people to feel that they are misfits. Did you know this? Very few feel that they fit into society. Everyone is saying, "I'm different from the others. They may or may not notice, but I

215

know that I'm different." And so everyone is like this—or at least a good part of the population. Some feel that it's okay for them to be different; others hate it; some don't care or think about it. But if asked, few would say, "I'm just an ordinary person, like everyone else."

Funny, isn't it, that everyone feels outcast to a certain degree, yet no one realizes that they are not the only ones? It's true that you may think of others as normal and you as different, but have you tried to see how everyone else is different from each other? Look at the people you know. Is anyone similar? Very few even resemble each other in character or personality. Few even like the same things. Yet no one notices this. Queer, is it not?

Deborah: That is definitely interesting. I just thought I hung out with people who were strange, like me.

Buddha: *Everyone thinks that. The only ones who do not think that they are different are the young children. They don't think about it at all. Young children (below the ages of four or five) do not even realize that there is a question like this. They assume that everyone is different. It's quite obvious to them. Do you remember being that age and knowing people? There weren't groups or cliques. There weren't in-crowds and out-crowds. You just met people— some you liked and some you didn't.*

Everyone wants to align with someone so that they do not think or feel like a stranger here on Earth. "If I align with this group I will be a part of something large, and my life will have meaning." Your life IS meaning. You don't need a group to be a part of life, or important to life. A small baby who lives for only a few months has a very large impact, and yet knows no one. We impact each other and life with our being, with our essence, and with our soul energetically.

Why do you want to belong?

Deborah: I don't quite know. I see that I want to feel the love of others around me and share in that love with them. I realize that being with people means learning, growing, and sometimes experiencing stress. I am sitting here, and although I'm lonely, I am not stressed. I don't have to impress anyone. I feel the love of nature. I watch the birds and talk to you. Still there's this need to share with someone.

Buddha: *There, you have said it yourself. You want to feel like you belong so you can share experiences and enjoy the love that stems from this. That is all. If you are not sharing, there's a feeling that you are not living. You are not fulfilling your purpose or performing correctly. The feeling that you have to be a part of something stems from your need to be loved and appreciated. That is the kind of sharing people want. If loving others is the motivation, you need not go anywhere. You can love the grocery checkout lady. You can love the little child you pass on your walk. You can love your neighbor as he mows the lawn. Love is not missing from your life. It is there for you to feel all of the time. You and others want to belong to a group or family so that you can receive the love from others. There's a feeling that by belonging, you'll receive love.*

When you don't belong, you don't have love in your life. This is the feeling, but it's incorrect.

Love is in your life at all times. If it doesn't come from another, it can come from you. It can come from within or without. You can bathe yourself in the aura of the love of the angels and Masters around you—around everyone. Love is all there is. Love surrounds you, is in you, and is a part of you. You belong here because you are a part of this love. Your group, or clique, is Planet Earth—humanity version. You are a part of the whole of humanity whether you choose to acknowledge your part in it or not.

There is also a need for stimulation. People like to be entertained. They go to parties, meet others for lunch, and watch TV or movies. Entertainment is essential to ego gratification and is a necessity for the happy monitoring of everyday events. Without entertainment you feel bored. Without entertainment life seems dry and listless.

So, are you thinking?

Deborah: Yes. I'm thinking that we often look at errands and sitting around watching the birds as nothing because there has been no noticeable entertainment. It seems like these interludes where we clean, take care of business, or buy groceries are merely gaps in the real parts of our lives, which are the "entertaining" parts. I see, however, that the errands could be as entertaining as the parties. We meet many people in our daily lives with whom we interact very little.

I find that my trips to the hair salon are rewarding. I know and enjoy the people there. Many grocery checkout clerks have been friendly, and I've enjoyed sharing energy with them. I meet many people daily and discount them because they don't belong to my "real" life. I see now that if I view every interaction as a loving connection, I will "belong" in my life at all times.

There is a feeling or sense that we haven't really connected meaningfully unless the relationship continues for a period of time. True, we learn and grow closer to others in time, but I've also found that I can be closer to some people in a moment than I am with others I've known for years.

I often go out to eat alone. People think this is terrible and that I must be so lonely. But I'm not. I meet and relate with the servers more than I normally would. I make more profound contact with everyone else than if I focused on one person sitting next to me. I also notice others in the restaurant and enjoy watching them interact, experiencing the energy in the room. I especially enjoy relating to infants in these settings. Most other people are ignoring the infants in the restaurant. The infants appreciate genuine eye contact and a warm smile. They light up and connect in a remarkable way.

Still there is the delight of sitting around with friends and sharing a warm and jovial conversation. These moments are like jewels.

Buddha, look at the birds flying and chirping. They're chasing and playing with each other in the sky. Do you hear them and see them?

Buddha: I hear and see them in a different way from you. It is not the same as when in a body. These are remarkable moments for you, as well, and as powerful and rejuvenating as conversations with friends. Do you feel the breeze?

Deborah: Yes, the temperature is perfect. A female cardinal just stopped by on the rail to say hello. A light breeze refreshes my skin like silk ever so gently being drawn across all the exposed parts of me. The air is full of bird sounds. I hear them calling and singing to each other, as is common in the evenings. The sun is within an hour of setting, and the light causes everything around me to appear bolder and richer in color. I smell a barbecue somewhere and imagine someone cooking for a family or friends. I see a little nuthatch sitting on top of a chimney, just looking around at the scenery. Great view, I imagine.

Buddha: Do you feel the love all around you?

Deborah: Yes, it is like a blanket of energy that surrounds me and is in me.

Buddha: Do you think that you would "belong" more on the planet with someone else sitting beside you?

Deborah: No, I feel complete and in harmony. I feel at peace.

Buddha: *Then that is "belonging" in the true sense. You are at one with all that surrounds you now. And some bird is noticing you and admiring your energy and the red color of your outfit—birds like color, you know. You've attracted several Cardinal admirers.*

Deborah: It's true. I'm wearing their color. I do feel an urge to speak, however—to communicate with someone.

Buddha: *Ah, now you're looking in a different direction. The urge you speak of is not the urge to be a part of a group. You feel the need to communicate and share information. You especially enjoy this. You also enjoy helping others and sharing information. It is your calling and your heart's wish. Most people enjoy communicating. It's an essential need. Do you feel you've been lacking in this?*

Deborah: I spend much time alone.

Buddha: *When were you alone this week? Even when you are home you spend a great deal of time on the phone.*

Deborah: I spoke to only a few people today.

Buddha: *There are few who enjoy the types of conversations that you do. Not many talk to the Buddha or want to know that you do. Is this not true? So you long for someone you can communicate with about this information, sharing insights and knowledge.*

Deborah: I'd love this.

Buddha: You've found some, have you not? Several others.

Deborah: Yes, but they are not here much.

Buddha: They will be more and more. Remember that your need for communication is real and necessary, but that your need is not met by communicating unnecessarily and by idle talk. You do not need this type of connection. Many people do. They do not feel the connectedness of the all in their everyday life, so they talk to others to feel this connection. You and others do not need this. You may need less communication than most because you are so well connected. Often you feel drained by talking to some people you do not enjoy. This is true for most people, and that is why they have short and superficial conversations. They do not relate to each other in the depths of their inner knowing. They do not want to. They are like the birds chirping to each other to remind each that they are present and a part of reality on this planet. If they are silent, they feel disconnected. Do you?

Deborah: No. Sometimes I feel more connected when I'm silent. It is then that I can pay close attention to what is going on around me. Sometimes conversation is distracting. Sometimes I speak to entertain or to be a part of the conversation. It's not normally pleasing, but it keeps things moving in a strange way. When I'm quiet, I hear more and am more in touch with others than when I'm speaking superficially. I do wish I had someone here to share in this beautiful evening. We wouldn't need to talk. It would be lovely to just share in the connectedness.

Buddha: Share with yourself. Share with your inner knowingness. See if that is not the same in some ways.

Deborah: Very much so. It feels as if I'm sharing with another. I feel complete. I don't need to go anywhere or do anything. I am not alone. I need nothing.

Buddha: Now you belong. Namaste, Deborah, until tomorrow.

Deborah: Thank you. Namaste.

My eyes fill with tears of gratitude and the remarkableness of the journey as I begin to reread what I've written tonight. Buddha began tonight with, "Today is the day you remember who you are." Though I didn't write my thoughts down, I was thinking something like, "I thought I knew who I was. And if I don't, how am I going to know in this one night?" He knew. He took me on a journey this evening and sitting here in my completeness, I do remember. I am. The moment is full and I watch as life unfolds moment by moment. The remarkableness of these great Masters astounds and touches me deeply. I sit with myself and am not alone. The "I" disappears and pure awareness remains—no identity; pure belonging.

The sun is near setting now. The branches of the pine above me are golden in color. The light shifts and the birds fly around me. I watch and enjoy, and still I communicate with you. Who are you? Namaste, my dear reader. The God in me honors the God in you. It is the same God. We are all God communicating with ourselves.

The spirit of the being known as Raphael

Purity of Mind, Body and Spirit

Deborah: I'm flying to California with my friend, **Gwen**, who has a question about purity of mind, body and spirit.

[**Gwen** asks the questions, the answers come to me, and I write them down.]

Gwen: I seem to get stuck in perfection, in other people's expectations, and in trying to help others. A different tact would be to live for myself and for my own purpose. When I've attempted to live for myself, I find it works well in my life. I wonder how to adapt what I'm doing for myself to a more global perspective in the long run.

Raphael: I am Raphael. I honor Gwen's question and will answer it for you. However, there is an underlying issue that she isn't addressing here. Her first question is, "What am I doing here?" It is in the context of this question that the other issues arise. If you are unsure of your mission in life, you will not know where you need to go and how to integrate who you are with your purpose and those around you.

Gwen : It's true that I tend to put pleasing other people first and their pleasure ahead of what I intend to do for myself. I know part of my mission, but the details allude me.

Raphael: So your mission then becomes pleasing other people. How are you fairing?

Gwen : Not well.

Raphael: You see that you are trying to change others. That is your mission. You seek to please them, which is the same as seeking to change them so they will be pleased. Their pleasure is pleasing to you, and so you ask them to provide this for you. You are failing because your mission (or attempted mission) is counterproductive to theirs. You cannot change them; you can only change yourself.

The only person you can actually please is yourself. When you attempt to change others, you fail. When you are pleased with yourself and act from your heart, you act in love. If others are open to accepting this love, you offer them a chance to have pleasure. Your aim, in this situation, is not to please them. You are pleasing yourself and therefore feeding those who wish to indulge in your aura of love and happiness.

So let's look at what your mission truly is, dear Gwen. Are you a healer or a missionary?

Gwen : I would say a little of both, but mainly a healer.

Raphael: It is true that you are a healer in a great sense. What is your aim in life? What is your joy?

Gwen : To create harmony.

Raphael: How do you do this?

Gwen : I bring together people of different ways and means in hopes they will learn to understand each other.

Raphael: Is this working?

Gwen : Yes, slowly.

Raphael: When has it worked best?

Gwen : In small groups and in unplanned events.

Raphael: Were you in control of these events? Did you mastermind the coexistence and cooperation?

Gwen : I was lead to these events, and my being there helped them to unite and achieve understanding.

Raphael: And how were you feeling at the time?

Gwen : Loving; open; in a listening mode.

Raphael: Were you listening to God and your Higher Self as well?

Gwen : Yes.

Raphael: Is it possible that your role as a healer is to lead by being lead? Can you imagine a life where you are not in control, but are open and loving and always where you need to be to promote healing? Is this a trend that's occurring in your life?

Gwen : So far, yes.

Raphael: Let's look at your original question now. You want to know about pleasing others, and I believe we've covered that. You cannot attempt to please them or to change them to be pleased. So you are correct in attempting to do what's best for you. However, you get confused when you attempt to control your own life in order to create what you think would be pleasing. When you let it all go and honor your Higher Self, following up with your understanding and gifts, you create great change in the world. Is this not remarkable?

So what is your mission in life? You already know it. It is to follow your heart and soul to promote higher learning and growth— to allow people to heal themselves and to heal the communications with each other. You are accomplishing this aim; however, you do not know how best to accomplish this in the future because you're creating in the moment. There is a higher plan and a direction you are taking. If you look at your life from an objective perspective, you will see a pattern. You can honor the pattern and move forward in *that direction, but you cannot predict the future or the outcome. You are on your path. When you are on the path of the soul, you see only as far as you need in order to accomplish your aim.*

As a spirit in a body you are required to accomplish a great many tasks. As a spirit you are able to access information that is not available on other levels—and you do this well. Also, you feel the need to control the body and the ego, to relate with other people, to honor others, and to honor yourself. You have a relationship with yourself that you are building as well.

Just as God split into parts as humans in order to relate to itself, you as humans split to see yourself in all of the different aspects that you are. So your mission, dear Gwen, is to understand and find glory in yourself. Your process will take you to the heights of healing and rejuvenation of the planet. You will only see as far as you need, and will only be given information as it is necessary. The rest is up to you. Just sit back, act in the moment, and enjoy the ride. You are the passenger as well as the person who steers. Learn to see who is in control. The passenger is not effective as a driver. Back seat drivers are never welcomed at any level. You can work from a soul level if you have faith and trust in yourself.

Trust is a major issue for most people. Learning to trust yourself to move in your body and to make your life profitable and healthy for yourself is a big assignment. Most accomplish this well. You are doing fine. Recognize this and you will have more faith in yourself. There will always be places of learning, but learn to be grounded in the success and not in the lessons. This is the heart of your question: *"Can I trust myself to be on my path?"* *The answer is yes, beyond a doubt.*

The spirit of the being known as Buddha

Neutrality; Time; Laughter

Buddha: Good evening.

Deborah : Hello, Buddha. It's a glorious evening.

Buddha: You are in good spirits. You have been neutral for most of the day. Are you having fun?

Deborah: I've had a delightfully fun day. And yes, I have been consciously and unconsciously neutral. I also noticed that I was kinder, sweeter, funnier and friendlier today. I enjoyed being with and connecting with other people. Even my errands were fun today, such as going to get gas and sitting in the car wash.

While I was living the day I didn't wonder if I was having fun. However, I did look back at times and realize that it was, indeed, a delightful day—quite the shift from yesterday. In fact, I realize as I write this that I woke up in a bad mood. I noticed this and shifted into neutrality. That's the last I remember of the bad mood.

Buddha*: Let's add another insight or step, shall we?*

Deborah : OK, count me in.

Buddha*: You're almost getting funny. And I noticed today that you were smiling and laughing a bit, too. Did I even spot you humming and singing a few times today? Yes, you were quite distracted from your serious question of whether you are fun and having fun.*

So let's look at something else I've noticed. You no longer worry about time. Is this not true?

Deborah : It is true. While I do look at the clock, I mostly pay attention to the feeling of when it's time to go or be somewhere. I've learned to feel when it's time for something—to go somewhere or to say something. (I finally learned that after many foot-in-mouth incidents.)

I also know that everything works out perfectly, though I may not know the plan. If something doesn't get done, someone doesn't show up, or I'm not at a place when I thought I was supposed to be, I know that it's not meant to be. Sometimes I even find out why and am always astounded at the synchronicity of life. I never grow tired of it or bored with seeing how life works so perfectly in sync.

Finally, if I know I'm supposed to accomplish something or be somewhere at a certain time, and it seems impossible to do, I change my view of the possible. I set my intention at designing the perfect brochure in four hours when it often takes me two days. I set my intention at arriving in ten minutes, or exactly at the correct time, when I'm twenty minutes away. This works 98% of the time. A creative rush will flow through me, or miraculously, I'm at the destination in half the time, and without driving faster than normal.

Now, if I could only get over my tension and irritation in traffic. I think a sign of true enlightenment is maintaining a calm acceptance of life while in traffic. I'm not there.

Buddha: We'll pray for you to the "car god."

Deborah : Thank you.

Buddha: You laugh, but you know, it could work. You have them. They're called police. I often see people praying when they see a police car—especially when they're driving very, very fast.

[We're both laughing now.]

Buddha: There isn't much to say when we're laughing, is there? We just can't think of anything serious to talk about. Are we missing the truth? If churches and temples were places where people came to laugh, would the truth be missed? Or, would it flow from the hearts through the laughter.

I'm speaking, of course, of loving laughter—not sarcasm or biting humor. Light-hearted, in-love-with-life humor, like we were enjoying. It is impossible to be out of the light of God when laughing in love. In fact, it's impossible not to feel love when laughing. Try it. Not negative humor, though, but positive fun and funnies. When you can laugh, if you can even smile, you are closer to God.

Namaste, Deborah. Sleep happily and in good humor.

APPENDIX

The following is a brief description the first seven chakras:

FIRST CHAKRA:
Location: Base of the spine
Element: Earth
Associated With: Survival and how comfortable we feel living on the planet
Function/Qualities: This chakra is concerned with shelter, food, rest, warmth and fear. It defines our understanding of whether or not we feel nurtured.
Other Qualities: Vitality groundingmaterial security, stability, primal trust courage, survival

SECOND CHAKRA:
Location: Lower abdomen, a couple of finger widths below the navel
Element: Water
Associated With: Sexuality, emotions, and family issues
Function/Qualities: Primal feelings, desire, sensuality, procreation, pleasure, relationships, openness to others, primal creativity clairsentience (sensitivity through feelings to others)

THIRD CHAKRA
Location: Solar plexus
Element: Fire
Associated With: Power, control, and manifestation in work
Function/Qualities: Personal powersocial identityautonomy authority, self-control, energy, will peace, radiance, self-acceptance, action, vitality

Fourth Chakra

Location: Heart, close to the sternum
Element: Air
Associated With: Love and the way one connects in relationship with
oneself
Function/Qualities: Compassion, warmth, sharing, devotion, uncon-
ditional and divine love and harmony

Fifth Chakra

Location: Throat
Element: Sound
Associated With: Communication and creative expression
Function/Qualities: Inspiration, confidence, independence, integrity

Sixth Chakra

Location: Center of the forehead—the "third eye"
Element: Light
Associated With: Intuition, clairvoyance and imagination
Function/Qualities: Idealism, concentration, peace of mind,
projection of will, manifestation

Seventh Chakra

Location: Top of the head
Element: Thought
Associated With: Wisdom, understanding and transcendent con-
sciousness
Function/Qualities: Divine purpose, universal consciousness,
enlightenment, unity with the Supreme Being